'Why are yo

'Isn't it obvious

'I wouldn't be asking you if it were.'

Mark Rowlands began to leaf silently through a sheaf of papers. Warily Tiffany watched him. Everything about the man bespoke toughness and hardness. A dangerous man, who would not hesitate to retaliate if he were crossed. In the circumstances it made no sense to Tiffany that there was a part of her that continued to find him enormously attractive.

Dear Reader

It's the time of year when nights are long and cold, and there's nothing better than relaxing with a Mills & Boon story! To help you banish those winter blues, we've got some real treats in store for you this month. Enjoy the first book in our exciting new LOVE LETTERS series, or forget the weather outside and lose yourself in one of our exotic locations. It's almost as good as a real winter holiday!

The Editor

Rosemary Carter was born in South Africa, but has lived in Canada for many years with her husband and her three children. Although her home is on the prairies, not far from the beautiful Rockies, she still retains her love of the South African bushveld, which is why she likes to set her stories there. Both Rosemary and her husband enjoy concerts, theatre, opera and hiking in the mountains. Reading was always her passion, and led to her first attempts at writing stories herself.

GAMES LOVERS PLAY

BY

ROSEMARY CARTER

MILLS & BOON

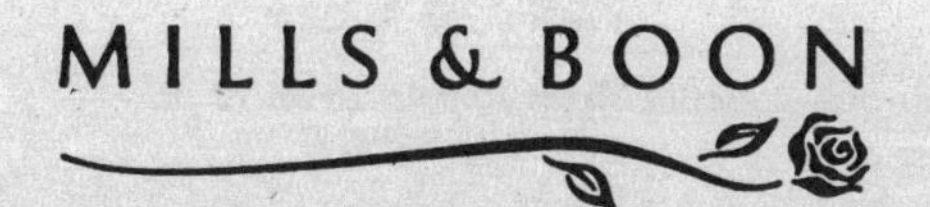

MILLS & BOON LIMITED
ETON HOUSE, 18-24 PARADISE ROAD
RICHMOND, SURREY TW9 1SR

All the characters in this book have no existence outside the imagination of the Author, and have no relation whatsoever to anyone bearing the same name or names. They are not even distantly inspired by any individual known or unknown to the Author, and all the incidents are pure invention.

First published in Great Britain 1994 by Mills & Boon Limited

This edition 1995

ISBN 0 263 78822 9

Set in Times Roman 10 on 11 pt.
01-9501-54880 C

Made and printed in Great Britain

CHAPTER ONE

THE bicycle came at her out of nowhere.

Later, when Tiffany returned to the scene, she would see the little alley at the side of the hotel, and would realise that the cyclist had come barrelling out of there and into the street. At the time, however, he seemed to have appeared out of nowhere.

She had just walked out of the swinging glass doors of the hotel and was stepping off the pavement into the street when he hit her. His wheel caught her shoe, knocking her to the ground with a force that knocked the wind out of her. She felt something dry and rather prickly on her face and hair, and she wiped it away with her hand.

'Don't you look where you're going, lady?' the cyclist yelled at her furiously, as he picked up himself, his bicycle and as much as he could of the litter of dried flowers which he'd been carrying in a basket at the front of the bicycle.

Tiffany looked at him helplessly, too winded to answer the accusation.

'Careless female,' the tirade continued.

'*You* were the careless one,' intervened the stern voice of a stranger. 'Riding along as if you owned the road.'

'My flowers,' the cyclist protested indignantly, in unconscious parody of Eliza Doolittle. 'The boss is gonna spit fire when he hears what happened. Who do you think's gonna make up the shortfall?'

'You will—if there's any justice in the world,' said the stranger cheerfully.

The cyclist glowered at Tiffany. 'She should have to pay.'

'If you don't look out, you'll pay for a darn sight more than a few damaged flowers,' the stranger advised him crisply. 'The lady might want you to make up the damage to her tights and her dress—not to mention her dignity.'

'Dignity—*hell*!'

A last malevolent glare at Tiffany. Then the cyclist, fearing perhaps that the stranger had the power to enforce his threat, swung his leg over the seat of his bicycle. Seconds later he had vanished in the traffic, leaving behind him as a kind of memento a scattering of dry red petals.

'Are you all right?'

Tiffany looked up at the stranger, who was bending over her now. He was very tall, she noticed, tanned and broad-shouldered, with dark hair that curled against the collar of his expensive jacket.

Tiffany nodded.

'Can you stand?'

It hadn't occurred to her that she was still on her knees. 'Oh, yes, I'm sure I can.'

She was making to get up when his hands reached for hers, and he drew her to her feet.

'Are you hurt?'

'I doubt it. I took a bit of a sprawl, but there are no bones broken, I'm sure of that.'

'Dignity a bit dented?'

She saw the way his eyes sparkled down at her—dark eyes, matching his hair, and fringed with impossibly thick lashes—and in a moment her own eyes sparkled back at him.

'Dignity, indeed! That was the word that got to the boy, didn't it?'

'Well—is it?'

'Dented? Of course not! It takes more than a mishap to dent my dignity—if I have any. None to stand on, anyway.'

Interest appeared in those dark eyes. 'Not all women treat themselves with as little seriousness as you seem to do.'

'It doesn't pay to, does it?'

'Maybe not.'

His hands were still holding hers, she noticed, with a strange quiver of pleasure. He was just inches from her—it was a long time since she had been this close to a man. With some surprise, she realised that she was enjoying the closeness.

'British?' he asked.

She smiled. 'Perceptive of you.'

'Hardly a difficult deduction—with the accent, and that dewy complexion, you'd have to be from England. And I get the feeling you haven't been in Zimbabwe very long.'

'Less than twenty-four hours.'

'Just long enough to have an accident. Are you staying in the hotel?' And when she nodded, 'Why don't you go back inside, clean up and take a bit of a rest in your room?'

The last words made Tiffany feel like some Victorian-era heroine: rather a nice feeling, when you came to think of it. Suppressing a smile, she said, 'I don't need a rest.' A glance at her watch then. 'Too late anyway; I have to be going.'

'Which way are you headed?'

Tiffany made a gesture.

'I'll see you across the street.'

'It really isn't necessary,' Tiffany protested, over the quite unjustified desire to remain a few moments longer in the company of this most attractive man. 'I've never before had a problem crossing the street.'

'I believe you, rose nymph.'

She was puzzled. '*Rose nymph*?'

'You collected some of your assailant's dry roses—or didn't you know?'

As he reached out and plucked something from her hair, Tiffany found that she had to make herself stand very still.

'I wouldn't like to see you knocked over again.' His grin was wicked. 'As a Zimbabwean myself, I'd hate to be responsible for another careless cyclist. Besides, you're a little pale, and we happen to be going the same way.'

With which he tucked his hand above her elbow and propelled her into the street. And once more Tiffany was conscious of an unfamiliar pleasure.

The street was wide. As they reached the other side, she danced her protector a smile. 'Thank you. That was very gallant of you.'

Dark eyes held her green ones for a long moment. 'If I didn't have an appointment to keep, I'd have asked you to have coffee with me.'

'That would have been nice,' she said, meaning it.

In fact, she was surprised to realise quite how much she would have enjoyed having coffee with the man.

She was about to walk away from him when he stopped her.

'Have dinner with me tonight.'

Something quickened inside Tiffany. With what mixed emotions she had left London just two days earlier, still very much saddened by Andrew's death, yet also somewhat excited at the thought of seeing the house he had left her. Knowing that there were things she must do, people she must see—the sinister Mark Rowlands for one—and not looking forward to any of it particularly.

Even her arrival in Bulawayo had not been auspicious. After a long and tiring trip she had arrived at the hotel where she had arranged accommodation, only to find that there'd been a mistake: the hotel was full, with not even one room to spare. It had taken a few phone calls on the part of a rather indifferent receptionist to find her a room elsewhere.

And now, unexpectedly, the tenor of the day had changed—she felt as if she'd been touched by adventure. An adventure of the nicest kind.

'Dinner sounds very nice,' she said with a smile.

'Eight o'clock suit you?'

'Eight is fine. I'll be in the foyer.'

'Perfect. Have to run. See you later.'

Tiffany watched the man stride away. He had vanished in the crowd, when she realised that she did not know his name.

Glancing at her watch, she knew that she would have to hurry too. Mark Rowlands was waiting for her, and something told her that the lawyer would not be impressed if she was late.

There was a restaurant on the corner, and she walked in and looked for a rest-room. When she had brushed the dust from her dress, she took a comb from her bag and began to neaten her hair.

There was a mirror on the wall, but it was spotted and old, so that she could only just make out her appearance: hair the colour of pale honey, falling in soft natural waves around her head, lips that curved easily in a smile, and her best feature, wide green eyes fringed with long lashes. Her dress was made of a soft lemon linen, very much more formal than her usual casual clothes. She had bought it in London, a day before catching the plane to Zimbabwe.

For some reason it had seemed important to make a good impression on Mark Rowlands. She thought of her correspondence with the lawyer who was dealing with Andrew's estate. The tone of his letters had made her a little uneasy: they weren't rude exactly, but frosty, just short of unfriendly. His last letter, written after she had informed him that she was flying to Zimbabwe, had contained no hint of a welcome.

Mark Rowlands... Once, long ago, Andrew had shown her a picture that had been taken years earlier, a group of family and friends. Shot awkwardly against the sun, the faces had been blurred and difficult to recognise. Tiffany had an idea that Mark Rowlands had been in that picture. A tall man, she thought now, about the same age as Andrew, probably in his mid-sixties, early seventies. And she wished that the picture had been clearer.

She was glad that she had thought of looking for the office building earlier. The entrance was at the end of the block. It was a newish building, all chrome and glass, with a smart-looking vestibule surrounding the row of lifts. Consulting a board bearing the names of lawyers, accountants and architects, Tiffany spotted the name at once—'Mark Rowlands and Associates, Suite 903'.

The reception area of Mr Rowlands's office was elegant too. Plush chairs, smoked-glass table with a stack of current magazines, good pictures hanging on the walls. Clearly Mark Rowlands and Andrew Donaldson had gone their different ways a long time ago. Apart from a few childhood memories, they could have had little in common.

The receptionist told Tiffany that the lawyer was waiting for her. She walked down a passage with doors on either side, and stopped beside the last door, the one with the name 'MARK ROWLANDS' emblazoned on it in neat bronze letters. She smoothed her hands over her dress, took a quick breath, then knocked on the door and walked inside.

Her eyes went first to the vacant chair behind the big mahogany desk. And then a movement drew her gaze to the window, and she saw a man standing there. A tall man. *The* man! The one who had helped her in the street.

For a few seconds they stared at each other in astonishment.

The man at the window recovered first. 'The rose nymph,' he said.

'*You are Mark Rowlands*?' The words burst happily from Tiffany's lips.

'As you must be Miss Tiffany Marlow.'

The formal note in his tone made Tiffany's head swing up. For the first time she saw that his eyes were hooded, without the welcome she expected. Tanned skin was stretched tautly over high-boned cheeks, and his lips were firmly set. She stared at him, bewildered, unable to understand why he was not as excited as she was by the coincidence.

Briskly he stepped away from the window and came towards her. An odd quiver ran through Tiffany as she looked into a face that was all hard lines and angles. If anything, he was even more attractive than she had realised.

'We never introduced ourselves.' His eyes raked her face.

'No...' Tiffany was uneasy now. 'You were walking away when I realised I didn't know your name.'

'It didn't matter, did it?' he observed mockingly. 'After all, we both knew we'd meet again tonight at the hotel.'

'Who'd have thought we'd meet again so soon?'

'I, for one, didn't. If I had, I wouldn't have——' He stopped abruptly, his lips even tighter. 'Sit down, Miss Marlow.'

Angry now, as well as bewildered, Tiffany sat down in the nearest chair. When Mark Rowlands had seated himself on the other side of the desk, he treated her to a long look. A look that was assessing, deliberate and insolent. Not a shred of fun or friendliness in him now.

'So, the rose nymph has turned out to be none other than Tiffany Marlow. The stranger from England who collects flowers in her hair. Why didn't I guess?'

A faint flush touched Tiffany's cheeks. To hide her nervousness, she clasped her hands firmly in her lap.

'Perhaps because you're staying in a different hotel from the one you mentioned in your letter,' Mark Rowlands answered his own question. 'What made you change your plans, Miss Marlow?'

The question had the sound of an accusation. Damn the man! Who did he think he was? Yes, she had written to him telling him where she would be staying, but it was none of his business if her plans had changed. His attitude was starting to annoy her intensely.

'The other place was full,' she informed him coolly. 'My reservation had been mislaid, and there wasn't another room to be had.'

'I see.'

'Come to that, I didn't guess too well either. It never occurred to me that the man who helped me on the street was the person I was coming to see. Even if I'd seen you entering the building, I'd never have taken you for Mark Rowlands. You...' She stopped.

'You were going to say?' he prompted politely.

'You're quite different from what I imagined.'

An autocratic eyebrow lifted. 'In what way?'

'I thought you were a contemporary of Andrew's.'

'You imagined I was in my sixties?'

'If not more.'

He grinned at that. Warmth lit his eyes and laughter-lines crinkled at the corners of his eyes and mouth, so that, just for a moment, Tiffany saw the ghost of the man who had plucked the dry rose petals from her hair.

'Thirty-three next birthday, Miss Marlow. Sorry to disillusion you.'

'Andrew had a photo... I thought I remembered a Mark Rowlands,' she said uncertainly. 'I guess I must have been mistaken.'

'Not necessarily. My father and I shared the same name.'

'Then he might have been the man in the photo?'

'Probably.' Dark brows drew together, and the laughter vanished from his eyes. 'I think it's fair to say that my mental picture of Tiffany Marlow was off the mark too.'

She looked at him curiously. 'Off the mark—in what way? Did you also think I'd be much older?'

His expression was derisive. 'You forget,' he said, 'I'm in possession of all Andrew's papers. I know exactly how old you are, Miss Marlow—twenty-four last March.'

Tiffany sat forward in her chair. Anger had caused her hands to tighten into fists, but she kept them out of sight on her lap, determined to keep her temper in check until she learned the reason for the lawyer's open hostility.

'Then my age isn't the problem,' she managed to say steadily. 'And yet, in some way, I've also surprised you, Mr Rowlands.'

'You could say that.' His tone was insolent. Lazy eyes searched her face.

'How?'

He did not reply right away. He simply sat there, watching her from across the desk. Holding his gaze, Tiffany thought back to the coolness of his letters.

'Are you going to tell me the problem?' she asked tensely.

His eyes were still on hers. 'The girl who was knocked down by the bicycle was very lovely. Spontaneous, fun, open. Incapable of scheming and manipulating—or so I'd have thought.'

A shiver ran through Tiffany, and the breath caught in her throat. 'Heavy words, Mr Rowlands. I don't like the tone of them.'

'No?' he drawled.

'No,' she told him decisively. 'You don't know me. Apart from those few minutes in the street, our only contact has been by way of letters. Why do you dislike me so much?'

'I haven't said that I do.'

'You haven't had to. Not twenty minutes ago you invited me to have dinner with you. You couldn't have been friendlier. And now I walk into your office, and the moment you realise who I am, your attitude changes. All of a sudden I've turned into some kind of villain. What's it all about, Mr Rowlands?'

'Really, Miss Marlow,' he said mockingly.

Tiffany's nails dug deep into her palms. 'You seem to think I should know what this is about. Well, I don't! Your letters came across as unfriendly, but I tried to tell myself I was imagining things, that brusqueness was your style. But now I'm here, and nothing has changed. *Why*, Mr Rowlands? Why are you so hostile?'

'Isn't it obvious?'

'I wouldn't be asking you if it were.'

'Really, Miss Marlow.'

'Say that again, and I'll get right up and walk out. It's quite clear you think badly of me, but you could tell me the reason.' As he still looked at her, she added, 'I've come a long way; you owe me that much.'

Mark Rowlands opened a folder that lay in front of him, and began to leaf silently through a sheaf of papers. Warily, Tiffany watched him. Everything about the man bespoke toughness and hardness. She sensed the ability to be ruthless, which she had not noticed at their very brief first meeting. A dangerous man, who would not hesitate to retaliate if he was crossed. In the circumstances, it made no sense to a furious Tiffany that there was a part of her that continued to find him enormously attractive.

'Suppose you tell me,' he said, in the contemptuous voice she was already beginning to dread, 'why Andrew Donaldson made you his beneficiary.'

She stared at him. 'Is that it?' she asked in amazement.

Mark Rowlands's expression did not change as he leaned back in his chair. 'I'm waiting.'

Tiffany hesitated a moment. 'I'm not quite sure how to answer the question—except that it was what Andrew wanted.'

'It's normal for a man to think of his family.'

'Andrew had no family, Mr Rowlands. His wife and child were killed years ago in a car accident. As his lawyer, you must know that.'

'No immediate family, Miss Marlow, but there are a few cousins, a nephew and two nieces.'

'With none of whom there was ever much contact. In all the time I knew Andrew, communication with his family never extended to more than a few obligatory Christmas cards.'

'Family all the same.' The lawyer was sitting forward now, his fingers interlaced on the desk.

Long fingers, Tiffany noticed, well-kept and strong. Sensuous fingers. She found herself reliving the feel of them on her bare skin.

She was unable to meet his eyes as she asked, 'Can't you accept the fact that it was Andrew's choice to leave his estate to me rather than to a collection of relatives who didn't mean much to him?'

Mark Rowlands was silent a few moments. Then he said, 'No, I can't.'

'Why not?'

'It's suspicious.'

'*Suspicious*!' Tiffany was outraged.

'Implausible. Wrong.'

Tiffany shook her head. 'That's ridiculous!'

'Is it? Is it really? What were you to Andrew, Miss Marlow?'

She looked at the square-jawed face. 'His employee. And his friend.'

'A very good friend, obviously.'

'Obviously.'

'Just a friend?'

'I resent the question.'

The lawyer was watching her in a way that unnerved her. 'I can't help wondering why you're so sensitive.'

'Don't bait me, Mr Rowlands,' Tiffany said furiously. 'I won't take it from you! You might as well tell me—is the family planning to contest the will?'

'Not any more.'

'In other words, they were thinking about it.'

'Naturally.'

'What made them decide against it?'

'There's no point in starting lengthy legal proceedings that have very little prospect of success.'

The statement should have cheered her. Tiffany had travelled a long way to inspect her inheritance. Since Andrew's family had no plans to contest his wishes, it was silly to let the disapproval of this very arrogant man get to her. But there it was, she did feel upset. More than that, she was distinctly uneasy.

Moving restlessly in her chair, she said, 'You're part of the family, I take it?'

Dark eyes glinted. 'No, I'm not. So if you're thinking that I was hoping to benefit by Andrew's will myself, you have it all wrong.'

That had, in fact, been Tiffany's thought.

'What was your connection with Andrew, Mr Rowlands?' she asked abruptly.

'He was my father's friend; they played cricket together when they were boys.'

'Why did he entrust his affairs to you?'

An amused look. 'Andrew knew that Dad's son was a lawyer. It's as simple as that.'

As simple as that. And yet not simple at all. Having met Mark Rowlands, it was hard to believe that shy Andrew Donaldson, a man possessed of such a fervent passion for privacy, would have chosen this autocratic man, the son of someone he had once known, to look after his affairs. Unless, of course, Andrew had been so certain that he would never return to Zimbabwe that he had felt his secret was safe. That must be it, of course.

'Don't tell them about me, Tiffany. I couldn't bear them to know. Promise me that you won't say a word...'

It was a promise that had meant everything to Andrew, and Tiffany had every intention of keeping it. She remembered how distressed he had been whenever he'd spoken about his family in Zimbabwe. No matter how hard she had tried, she had never quite been able to convince him that his family would know nothing about him. Again and again, he had asked for reassurance.

Mark Rowlands was leafing through the bundle of papers once more. When he looked up again his eyes were narrowed and thoughtful.

'For the last three years, all of Andrew's correspondence was handled by you.'

Why was he persisting with this inquisition? Anyone listening to him would think Tiffany had committed some heinous crime.

Meeting his gaze head-on, she said, with a calmness she was far from feeling, 'That's right.'

'Why?'

'It was the way he wanted it.'

'Correspondence regarding his money, his property, all the stocks and shares he'd inherited from his father.'

'Yes.'

'Everything controlled by you, Miss Marlow.'

'*Wrong*! I did not control Andrew's affairs!' Tiffany threw the words at him vehemently.

'No?'

'No. It's true that I looked after his correspondence. But whenever I wrote to you, I was simply following his instructions.'

'Instructions manipulated by you?'

His insolence was deliberate, and it brought a flush to her cheeks. '*How dare you*?'

'I dare because I find the circumstances a little too strange.'

'You weren't there, Mr Rowlands.'

'Precisely why I want you to explain things to me.'

'There's nothing *to* explain.'

'Was Andrew ill?'

'No!'

'Disabled in some way?'

She thought. If only you hadn't made me give you that promise, Andrew. You had nothing to be ashamed of.

'Good heavens, no,' she said briskly. 'There was nothing the matter with Andrew's faculties. He was an intelligent man, he always knew exactly what he wanted.'

'Then why do I get the impression that you controlled his life?'

'I tell you, you have it all wrong. Whatever I did was always in accordance with his wishes.'

'I only have your word for that.'

'Do you think I'm a liar?' she asked furiously.

'Would I be wrong if I did?' he drawled.

'Damn right you would be, Mr Rowlands!' Tiffany paused a few seconds. She took a deep breath before continuing in a quieter tone, 'I wasn't the first person to take charge of Andrew's correspondence. Before me there was a woman by the name of Agnes Winton. And before her, someone else.'

'I remember.'

'Did you think of them as being dishonest and manipulative as well?'

'No.'

'Why not?'

'Neither of them were beneficiaries of Andrew's will.'

Tiffany sat upright on the edge of her chair, the toes of her new patent-leather shoes digging into the thick carpet. She had been looking forward so much to seeing Zimbabwe. For a short while, Mark Rowlands had made her feel as if she were on the verge of adventure. The same man was now threatening to sour her visit.

'You make it sound so sordid,' she whispered.

'The *sole* beneficiary,' the lawyer said pointedly.

'You've no right to do this to me.'

'Andrew's will was drawn in England by a lawyer named Barnett.'

'That's right.'

'Did you tell him how it should be drawn?'

'I did not!' She glared at him. 'You don't believe me, do you?'

'You've said nothing to convince me that I should.'

Tiffany's gaze went to a paperweight on the desk, a pretty thing made of glass shot with wisps of colour. She was sorely tempted to hurl it at Mark Rowlands's head.

'I wouldn't advise it,' a dry voice warned.

'You're safe, I'm not violent.' Alarmed by the intensity of her reaction, Tiffany tried to make herself sound indifferent. 'Look, Mr Rowlands, I don't know what else I can say. Either you believe me or you don't. It doesn't matter to me either way.'

The lawyer did not answer her. He only looked at her, speculatively, searchingly, as if his eyes could penetrate to the very core of her being.

All at once, Tiffany had had enough. 'How long will it take to wind up the estate?'

'It all depends.'

'On what?' she asked tautly.

'What you decide to do with the house, for one thing. I presume you'll want to sell it.'

'I won't know that until I see it.'

'Oh?'

'I thought you understood my reason for coming here.'

'There are things I understand about you, Miss Marlow.'

Tiffany shoved back her chair and rose quickly to her feet. 'Given your hostility, I'll find another lawyer to handle the estate.'

Mark Rowlands laughed. 'You will find, Miss Marlow, that even you, with all your ingenuity, have certain limits.'

'Meaning?' she asked coolly.

'The house is yours; you can do with it whatever you like.'

'I know that.'

'The money is another matter.'

Tiffany's hands went to the back of the chair, gripping it tightly. 'What are you trying to tell me?'

'The money is in trust.' Sensuous lips lifted at the corners, and the dark eyes gleamed. Mark Rowlands paused a long moment, and Tiffany had the feeling that he was quite deliberately keeping her in suspense.

'I am not only the executor of Andrew's estate, I am also the trustee of your money,' he said then.

Tiffany trembled as she looked at him. These were not the facts as she thought she knew them.

'I don't believe you...'

'I'm a lawyer, Miss Marlow. Whatever my personal feelings about you, I wouldn't mislead you.'

'But Andrew...' She stopped.

'Andrew may have had second thoughts. Or perhaps his English lawyer, Barnett, did. Perhaps he convinced Andrew not to let you have your way with his money after all. Here—you can see for yourself.' With which Mark Rowlands pushed the will to her side of the desk.

It did not take Tiffany long to read it. And she remembered a day when Mr Barnett had phoned Andrew. A longish conversation, she recalled. She'd heard

Andrew's voice, raised in unaccustomed anger, as if the lawyer were telling him something he did not want to hear. Afterwards, he had seemed unhappy. He had not told her what the conversation was about, and it had not occurred to her to ask.

Looking up again, she found the lawyer watching her. Feeling a little ill, she said, 'You could let someone else take over.'

'No.'

'But, Mr Rowlands——'

'Absolutely not.' His tone was crisply decisive, leaving her in no doubt that he was not a man to be easily swayed.

'Why not?' she asked slowly, knowing she had to try anyway.

'I consider myself responsible for what happens to that money. Andrew's father worked very hard to accumulate it, and I have no intention of letting an unscrupulous opportunist have her way with it now.'

'Does this mean I need your permission whenever I want to spend something?'

'It does.' His voice was butter-smooth.

Tiffany bit down hard on her bottom lip, willing herself not to tremble. When she could talk, she said, 'Don't you realise that I can't bear the thought of having to see you again?'

He laughed, and this time he sounded genuinely amused. 'Unless you decide to waive all claim to Andrew's estate, you don't have any other option.'

It was still very hot when Tiffany left the office building. At the corner she stopped, watching the traffic light turn to green and the people gathered there begin to cross the road. Everyone seemed to have a destination. Everyone except for Tiffany.

Excitement had carried her along the city streets that morning. Andrew had told her so much about the continent and the country of his birth. For years she had longed to see Zimbabwe for herself. And now, here she was. *Africa—at last*! she had told herself that morning while pausing to examine the colourful beaded offerings of a street vendor, or listening to a spirited group beating out a rhythmic tune on home-made instruments.

That exhilaration was now gone. After her encounter with Mark Rowlands she felt curiously empty, drained of her earlier eagerness to explore. At the same time, she could not bear the thought of her impersonal hotel room.

Halfway down the block a few people were boarding a bus. Impulsively, Tiffany ran to join them. She had no idea where the bus was going; she did not care.

She sat down next to a woman who was so laden with parcels that Tiffany had to perch on the edge of the seat. Three stops further on the woman left the bus, and Tiffany took her place.

Suddenly they had left the downtown area and were in a residential suburb. The streets were wide, bright and attractive in the sunlight. Pushing Mark Rowlands firmly from her mind, Tiffany stared out of the window. She was in Africa. With no idea how long she would be here, it was up to her to enjoy every minute of her time.

The bus stopped again. People were standing in the aisle, ready to disembark. Tiffany stood up too.

As the bus pulled away, Tiffany watched a group of schoolchildren go down the street, swinging their satchels and talking animatedly as they went. She decided to follow them. When they turned a corner, she turned it too.

Seconds later, the children were forgotten as she gazed about her, entranced. Vivid colour everywhere—bougainvillaea climbing roofs and trees and cascading over garden walls in flamboyant shades of red and purple and orange, scarlet hibiscus, jasmine, filling the air with a heady sweetness. The rampant lushness surprised

Tiffany, for she knew that most of southern Africa was in the grip of a vicious drought. Evidently there were shrubs that did not need much water to survive.

She did not know how long she walked through the hot streets, drinking in a scene that was altogether different from the tranquil English village where she'd lived with Andrew.

She stopped when she came to a garden with a low wall, and saw a little stone frog at the edge of a pond, a frog that might have been the twin of the one in Andrew's garden. The pond was empty. In a time before the drought, water must have cascaded from the frog's mouth, but there was no water now. Tiffany did not notice these details as she was swept by a wave of homesickness and grief.

Eyes turning inwards, she thought of Andrew. Andrew Donaldson . . . frail and weather-beaten, with hands like knotted ropes, and a kind and gentle face.

'My family must never know about me,' he had said, his expression haunted.

'Would it make any difference to them if they did?'

'Knowing that I can't read or write? Yes, Tiffany, it would make a difference.'

'It's no crime,' she said softly. 'Just because there wasn't much in the way of remedial teaching when you were young, it doesn't make you any less intelligent than the next person. Besides, Andrew, you *can* read. You can write too.'

'Very little, no more than a six-year-old. Not enough to get by. The fact is, I don't want them to know, Tiffany. It's the reason I never went back to Zimbabwe—Rhodesia as the country was called back then, when I left it. They'd look down on me, all that lot, I know they would. Besides, there's nothing there for me now—only the property and some money, and without my wife and child that doesn't mean anything.'

'Andrew . . .' Tiffany had said, seeing his grief.

'Losing Amy and little May in the accident was the worst thing that ever happened to me. At the time, I thought I'd never get over the loss, but somehow I did manage to find contentment of a sort again. I haven't wanted more than the garden and the horses and the stables. And now you're here, Tiffany, and though nobody could ever make up for Amy and May, you've given me happiness.'

'I love it here, Andrew. You helped me through a bad time too.'

'You'll get whatever I have, Tiffany. You know that, don't you?'

'It isn't necessary,' she had protested, not for the first time. 'I'm only an employee.'

'You stopped being an employee long ago, my dear.'

'Your family may not like it.'

'Family?' he had repeated, on a note of unaccustomed bitterness. 'A few formal notes when my wife and child died. Duty Christmas cards. No other contact. You call that family?'

'Even then... You shouldn't be leaving it all to me.'

'It's the way I want it, Tiffany. You'll let Barnett have the instructions?'

She remembered the stubbornness in his voice. Gentle man that Andrew had been, once a decision was made, he almost never changed his mind.

'What will you do with the house in Zimbabwe, Tiffany?'

'I don't want to think about it,' she'd said abruptly. 'You're going to be around for a long time yet.'

'No, girl, we both know that's not true. Not now... Sell the place or keep it, it's yours to do with as you like. Only promise me that you won't tell any of them my secret.'

'You have my promise,' she had reassured him.

CHAPTER TWO

THE sound of the telephone shattered the silence. Tiffany jerked up in surprise.

Putting down the room service menu which she had been studying without much enthusiasm, she picked up the receiver. Must be the front-desk receptionist wanting to clarify some detail of her stay, she thought.

'Hello?'

'Rose nymph?' came a familiar voice. It sounded surprisingly cheerful.

Tiffany caught her breath. Then she said stiffly, 'Why, Mr Rowlands...'

'How very formal,' he mocked.

'Polite is the word.'

'Rather grimly so. Tell me, rose nymph, are you always unpunctual?'

'Not as a rule.'

'It's ten past eight—we were supposed to meet in the foyer at eight.'

Tiffany pushed a hand through her tousled hair, the movement bringing her face to face with the mirror. She was wearing no make-up, and it was so hot in the room that her skin glistened with perspiration.

'Still there?' Mark Rowlands asked, as she made a grimace at her reflection.

'I haven't slammed down the phone on you yet, have I?'

'I take it you were delayed. That you'll be down in a few seconds.'

'I won't be down at all,' she said flatly.

'Something better come up? Or had you forgotten our date?'

'Actually,' Tiffany said, with another harassed glance in the mirror, 'I hadn't given it a thought.'

'After only one day in the country, you're already so swamped with admirers that you don't take your social arrangements seriously?'

It so happened that Tiffany could not remember the last time she'd been out with a man. After Wayde had double-crossed her without any sign of remorse, she had never accepted another date. Andrew, gentle undemanding Andrew, whose only interest in her had been protectively fatherly and wholly platonic, had been the sole man in her life for three years. And what would Mr Rowlands, with his wretched opinion of her, say to that?

'When I make an arrangement I keep it every time,' she said evenly.

'Why aren't you in the foyer now, in that case?'

'Because,' Tiffany said slowly, 'it didn't occur to me that we still had a date.'

'We'd arranged it.'

'Yes, I know.' The teasing note in his voice was disturbing. Far easier to think of Mark Rowlands as the arrogant lawyer of their second meeting than as the too-attractive man who had helped her in the street. 'But that was before...'

'Before what?' he asked with mock interest.

Hating him for the game he was playing with her, Tiffany's fingers tightened on the receiver. 'Before we talked in your office.'

'I don't remember a change in plans.'

'There wasn't one—not in words anyway.'

'There wasn't one at all. I think you should come down and join me, Tiffany.'

Tiffany... How odd her name sounded when he spoke it. It was more than his accent, which was pleasant and broad, a little like Australian, yet different. She had the strangest feeling that her name would never sound quite the same on any other man's tongue.

'No,' she said, with an attempt at firmness. 'Things *have* changed, Mr Rowlands. You've made no secret of the way you regard me: you couldn't think much worse of me if you tried. Why on earth would you want to waste an evening having dinner with a scheming manipulator?'

'Ah, but the date I made was with a laughing English nymph.'

'Stop taunting me, Mr Rowlands!'

'A girl with dried flowers in her hair,' he continued, as if he had not heard her protest. 'And, by the way, my name is Mark.'

She could not prevent the laughter that cascaded, clear as a bell, through the telephone line. 'You're quite a charmer, aren't you, Mark?'

He laughed too. 'Five minutes.'

'I'm not dressed for dinner.'

'Ten.'

'I haven't unpacked.'

'Any more excuses, Tiffany, or will fifteen minutes be enough for you?'

'There's really no point in this.'

'What did you plan to do about a meal?'

Tiffany was silent as she scowled down at the menu in her hand.

'Room service, Tiffany? A tray on your bed?'

She had read through the menu three times without finding a single item that appealed to her. If she ordered at all, it would be only because she had barely eaten all day, and was hungry.

'Something like that,' she admitted.

'I'll be waiting for you in the foyer.'

'I haven't said that I'll come.'

'I can offer you a mushroom steak that will make your mouth water. Delectable wine made from grapes grown on the other side of the Limpopo River.'

Arrogant man that he was, he was succeeding in tempting her.

'Are you going to tell me you look forward to spending your first evening in Zimbabwe alone?' he persisted.

She closed her eyes. 'Not exactly.'

'There's your answer, then.'

'We won't enjoy the meal, Mr Rowlands.'

'Mark. Do you always play hard to get, Tiffany?'

She took another rueful look at herself. 'The circumstances are unusual.'

'You'll regret it if you don't join me.'

'*You* may think I'll regret it, but that's only because you're an arrogant man, Mark Rowlands. Autocratic, self-opinionated, thoroughly disagreeable.'

'Good grief! All that?'

'I don't see how we can possibly get through an evening without an argument.'

'Do I hear a smile in your voice, Tiffany?'

Yet another look in the mirror. Her lips were, in fact, curling up at the corners. She wondered how he could tell through the telephone line.

'I guarantee you a good time, Tiffany.'

She did not doubt that he would keep his word. If she joined him tonight he would tease her, charm her, woo her with his silver-tongued magic. But tomorrow... Ah, tomorrow would be different. Reality would have returned. Tiffany would be once more the manipulating she-devil, Mark Rowlands the relentless lawyer, and Tiffany would feel let down and upset. More than that, she would be furious with herself for giving in to him.

'This is silly,' she said slowly. 'You know very well that our relationship has changed since we made the arrangement.'

'We can change it back.'

'Permanently?' she asked disbelievingly.

He paused, and she was as aware of his hesitation as if he had been in the room with her.

'For this evening,' he said then, and Tiffany expelled the breath she had not known she was holding.

'That isn't good enough,' she said flatly.

'Why not? For a few hours you'll be the rose nymph once more, and I'll be the nameless stranger.'

'No, Mark, because we'll both know better. You'll see me as the bitch who talked poor Andrew into leaving her everything he owned. And I'll see you as the beastly lawyer who refuses to hear the truth.'

'We can make-believe otherwise, Tiffany, even if it's only for a short time.'

'Children play make-believe games,' she said harshly.

'Adults play games too.'

'This is ridiculous...' she said, and wished that she weren't quite so tempted.

'Adults play more exciting games than children. Perhaps because adults understand that the games aren't real, and that gives them an extra thrill.'

There was a seductive quality in his voice now, and it filled Tiffany with ripples of unaccustomed sensation. Instinct told her to hang up on Mark quickly, to put a stop to his nonsense while she could still say no to him.

She looked around her—and that look was her undoing. She saw the heavy rug, the dowdy curtains, the mass-produced flower pictures, the depressing sterility of the hotel room. The only thing that made the room human was the suitcase at the foot of the bed, clothes spilling out of it because Tiffany had lacked the energy to unpack. That was what she would do tonight, she told herself. She would unpack, organise her possessions, wash her hair, iron some clothes and make detailed notes in preparation for her next battle with Mark Rowlands.

'Twenty minutes?' she heard him ask softly.

The sterility of the room got the better of her. She took a breath, and said, 'Give or take a few.'

Tiffany saw Mark the moment she stepped out of the lift. He came to meet her, taller than every other man in the place, lithe and broad-shouldered, far more good-looking than he had a right to be. In his office, in his expensive three-piece suit, he had been very much the sophisticated lawyer. The casual navy blazer and white trousers he wore now gave him a slightly rakish look.

Looking down at her, he said, 'Hello, rose nymph,' and his eyes swept over her in a way that told Tiffany he was taking in every detail of her appearance. It was a particularly male kind of look, one that struck a chord somewhere deep inside her, and suddenly she was glad that she had decided to wear another one of her new London dresses, a soft lilac jersey that moulded itself to the shape of her body. The heavy silver bracelet which had belonged to her mother was on her wrist, and in her ears were the dangling earrings which Andrew had bought for her at a local fair. She had even managed to wash her hair.

'Not bad for twenty minutes,' Mark commented.

'Does that mean you approve?' She danced him a look, and realised she was flirting with him.

His eyes glinted with answering devilment. 'I can think of several women who take two hours to get ready—and don't look anywhere near as good.'

Several women... But why was she surprised? A man like Mark Rowlands would hardly have reached the age of thirty-two without women in his life. How many really didn't matter to her, Tiffany told herself firmly. This dinner had been arranged before each had known the identity of the other; obviously it had tickled Mark's particular sense of humour to stay with it. And maybe there was nothing wrong with that. Hereafter, they would see each other only in his office, but was there any harm in a respite from an otherwise acrimonious relationship?

She'd thought they would eat at the hotel and was surprised when he took her arm and led her towards the street.

'There's a perfectly good restaurant right here,' she protested.

'There's an even nicer one somewhere else.'

Mark's car—sleek, sporty and expensive—matched its owner. The restaurant he took her to was elegant too. Old-world maps decorated the timber-panelled walls, and copper lamps hung low over damask-covered tables. When the waiter had taken their order—the mushroom steak Mark had tempted Tiffany with earlier, and the wine—Mark said, 'Tell me about yourself.'

She shot him a spirited look. 'You have the complete low-down on me already.'

'There must be a few remaining facts that I don't know.' His grin was unrepentant.

'Are you asking me to condemn myself further?'

'Would it be condemnation?'

Tiffany could have risen to the bait, but she understood that this was not the man she had done battle with earlier in the day. He was teasing her, but he also looked genuinely interested.

And so she told him about herself. Not everything, of course. She omitted the bit about Wayde, who had hurt her so badly in the weeks before they were to have been married that for a time she had been filled with hopelessness. She told him about a childhood spent on a farm not far from the ocean, about the mother who had given her a love of music and nature, and the father who had taught her to ride a horse almost as soon as she could walk. She talked about her life with Andrew.

'He knew everything there was to know about horses. You should have seen his stables, Mark—people were prepared to pay whatever he asked for the privilege of leaving their horses with him. He gave lessons, and he trained horses too. A horse trained by Andrew Donaldson was an animal worth having.'

'You make him sound quite a man, Tiffany.'

'The finest one I ever knew.'

'I'm sorry I never met him.'

'Yes, well...'

They were getting into dangerous territory. Tiffany wished that she had left Andrew out of her story.

'I don't understand why he never came back to Zimbabwe,' Mark said.

Tiffany shifted in her chair. Now, more than ever before, she understood why her dear friend had been so insistent that his problem be kept a secret from all the people he had once known. Successful in his own world, Andrew Donaldson would have been uncomfortable in the company of a man like Mark Rowlands. If the members of Andrew's family possessed even a shadow of Mark's sophistication, he would have been uncomfortable with them too.

'Andrew had made a life for himself in England,' Tiffany said, a little too abruptly.

'But never to return to the place where he was born. If only for a visit?'

'He...wasn't much of a travelling man.'

Tiffany moved her eyes from Mark's. She had made Andrew a promise, and she meant to keep it. And she knew that Mark, astute lawyer that he was, would have noted the evasiveness of her answer.

'Did you love him?' Mark asked, in a tone that forced her to look back at him.

'I adored him,' she answered, without hesitation.

'Your address was the same as his.'

Tiffany sat up straighter in her chair. 'That's right.'

'You lived with him.'

'We lived in the same house,' she said levelly.

'Just the two of you?'

'Just the two of us.'

'In the same bedroom?'

'Separate bedrooms,' she told him crisply.

'For the sake of appearances?'

'Appearances never came into it. We've been over this before. Andrew was my employer. He was also my very good friend.'

'As well as your lover?'

Tiffany shot up from her chair. Mark's hand caught her wrist before she could move away from the table.

'Sit down.' Authority in the low voice.

'No...'

'Sit,' he ordered.

Sensuous fingers sent ripples of sensation coursing up Tiffany's arm, so that, for a moment, she felt a little dizzy. She was angry too, but the restaurant was crowded, and she knew that to continue defying Mark meant creating a scene. She hated scenes.

He was still holding her wrist as she sank back in her chair. Through her teeth, she said, 'You can let go now, I won't run away.'

He held her wrist a second longer before releasing it. Oddly, where his fingers had been, her skin was suddenly cold.

'This was a mistake,' she said quietly. 'I should never have let you talk me into going anywhere with you. Take me back to the hotel.'

'When we've finished our meal.'

'Now.'

'No, Tiffany.'

'If you won't drive me, I'll call for a taxi.'

'I'll drive you myself—but not yet.'

Her eyes sparked angry fire at him. 'I'll only stay on one condition.'

'Which is?'

'Not another word about my life with Andrew.'

'Difficult,' he said, 'given the fact that without Andrew you would not be in Zimbabwe.'

'Not another word about him *in this restaurant*.'

He was quiet a few seconds, his gaze on her face, lingering on angry eyes, on lips that trembled slightly, descending to the spot where her pulse beat at the base of her throat.

'Condition accepted,' he agreed at last.

They ate in silence for a while. And then, unexpectedly, Mark began to talk, telling Tiffany about himself. Like her, he had grown up on a farm, a tobacco farm. It had never occurred to him that he would be anything but a farmer himself, until the day his father had been involved in a lawsuit. The young Mark had accompanied his dad to court every day, and had been enthralled by the drama of the proceedings. By the time the trial had ended, he had made up his mind about his future career.

The tension began to drain from Tiffany as she listened to him talk. He told her about judges and juries, and cases he'd fought over the years. He spoke interestingly and well, bitingly crisp one minute, amusing the next. Despite her resolve to remain cool with him, she found herself laughing more than a few times.

'Has your profession had all the drama you expected?' she asked, when he paused to sip his wine.

Mark grinned, his teeth white against his tan, attractive lines crinkling around his mouth and eyes. 'It's had its moments.' He picked up the menu and passed it to her. 'You must be tired of listening to me—what do you fancy for dessert, Tiffany?'

It was quite late when they left the restaurant. After three glasses of excellent wine, Tiffany was feeling pleasantly mellow.

She did not know how long they had been driving when she realised that it had been a while since she had seen houses and street-lights and cars. Looking out into the unlit darkness, she suddenly sat up with a start.

'Where are we, Mark?'

'Does it matter?'

'Where are you taking me?' she demanded.

'You'll find out in good time.'

'We've left the city. We have, Mark, haven't we?'

'Yes.'

'I insist on knowing where we're going!'

When he did not answer, she tried to read his expression, but it was too dark in the car to see anything more than the outline of a strong profile.

As her mother's long-ago warnings about being careful with strangers came back to her, Tiffany was suddenly frightened. 'I shouldn't have let you talk me into going out with you tonight.'

'Oh?'

'I don't know a thing about you.' Apart from the fact that he was the son of Andrew's friend, and more devastatingly attractive than she had ever dreamed a man could be.

'I'd have thought that after several hours of non-stop conversation you know quite a lot,' Mark drawled.

Tiffany's lips tightened grimly. 'You might as well understand that if you have any thoughts of a one-night stand, you can forget them.'

'Why is that?'

'I'm not the type,' she said, as convincingly as she could.

Mark laughed, the sound low and attractive in the purring car. Too primitively dangerous. 'I wouldn't do anything you didn't want to do too, Tiffany. I'm certainly not a murderer or a rapist.'

'Mark...'

'Relax and enjoy the drive.'

But Tiffany was unable to relax. The wine-induced mellowness vanished as she sat rigidly in her seat and stared out into the darkness. The vastness of the countryside was unlike anything she had ever known. There were no little villages, no lights shining invitingly in windows. Now and then, in the distance, she would see a farmhouse, but the houses were disturbingly far apart. Few cars were on the road. The general sense of distance and isolation made Tiffany feel more uneasy by the moment.

And then Mark was turning off the road, and down what appeared to be a narrow lane. Tiffany stared at him. As if sensing her gaze, he turned his head and grinned, his teeth gleaming white in the darkness.

Moments later the headlights of the car picked out a house. Not one light shone in the windows.

Tiffany's breath grew shallow with tension. When she turned to Mark once more, it was an effort to make her voice sound assertive. '*This* is where you're taking me?'

'This is it,' he said mockingly.

She gave a violent shake of the head. 'Forget it! Take me right back to the city.'

'Not yet, rose nymph.'

'Immediately!'

But Mark was already getting out of the car. Seconds later, he was at her side and opening her door. 'Come,' he said, and reached for her hand.

Tiffany drew back. 'I suppose this is some trysting-place to which you bring all your women? You're wasting your time, Mark Rowlands. I thought I'd made it clear that I don't go in for one-night stands.'

'Neither do I,' came his unexpected response. His hand was still reaching for her.

She ignored it. 'What is this place?'

He took his time about answering, thereby increasing the suspense.

When he did speak, Tiffany heard laughter in his voice. 'Actually—it's Andrew's house.'

Tiffany jerked in her seat. '*Andrew's house*...?' The words skittered on her tongue.

'Your house now. Funny, I thought you might have guessed where we were going. Now will you get out?'

She left the car on a wave of excitement. In wonder, she stared at the dark bulk in front of her, scarcely able to believe that what she was seeing was really her house. *Her house*. It was so much bigger than she'd expected. More isolated too.

'Why didn't you tell me where you were taking me?' she asked animatedly.

'I wanted it to be a surprise.'

'It's such a long way out of Bulawayo, Mark. How far is it?'

'About fifty miles. Not far by African standards.' He sounded amused.

'Why is it so dark? Who lives here? Won't they mind us barging in on them like this?' One after another, the questions tumbled from her lips.

'Nobody lives here; the place is empty,' Mark told her.

Until today, the house Tiffany had inherited had been a nebulous thing in her mind, a place with no actual substance. Now that she was here at last, there was so much she needed to know.

'Andrew was born here,' Mark said.

'Yes...'

'His father lived in the house most of his life. When he died, and Andrew showed no interest in coming back to live here himself, the place was rented out. The last tenants moved out a few months ago.'

'I can't wait to see it!'

Mark laughed, the sound vital and very attractive. 'This is the first time I've seen you so excited.'

Tiffany laughed too, more softly. 'Is there some way we can get inside?'

'Do you think I'd have driven you out all this way without bringing a key?'

Mark put out his hand again, and this time Tiffany took it. She was elated as they walked along an uneven path towards the house. The air was alive with the shrilling of crickets, heady with the perfume of some tropical shrub.

She gasped when they came to the house and Mark shone a light over a tall wooden door.

'You didn't tell me you had a torch—you could have lit up the path,' she accused.

'I could have.'

'Why didn't you?'

'I enjoyed holding your hand.'

In the darkness, Mark's laughter was so erotic that something deep inside Tiffany came to life, a feeling that was raw and primitive, an emotion she did not care to acknowledge. If there was one man she did not want to get excited about, it was Mark Rowlands. With Wayde she had never anticipated heartbreak; if she was not extremely careful, Mark could cause her to plunge headlong into it.

'Did it bother you so much?' he asked.

It was difficult to speak. 'I want to see my house,' she said, to evade the question.

Mark turned the key in the lock. Then he pushed the door open, standing aside to let Tiffany walk past him.

This moment should be special, she thought. The first time across the threshold of the house she had travelled so far to see. Yet, absurdly, she was less aware of the house than of the tall man just behind her.

They stood together in silence, the space between them charged with a peculiar tension. A few seconds went by. Then Tiffany took a deliberate step away from Mark.

'Where is the light switch?' she asked tautly.

'Behind you. Problem is, the electricity's been disconnected.'

'Pity—I'd have liked to see inside.'

She had turned back to the open door, when Mark touched her arm. 'We have the torch,' he reminded her, swinging it in an arc. 'It's not very much, but it will give you some idea of the place.'

The torchlight lit up only a small area; beyond its glow the darkness was intense. When Mark reached for Tiffany's hand once more, she let him have it without protest.

He led her into a room with a wide floor and big windows. The living-room, Tiffany thought, as the torchlight performed a provocative dance, darting here and there, picking out strange shapes and shadows.

'Romantic' was the word that popped into her mind without volition. With the right person, she amended firmly, seconds later. Romance could only flourish in the company of the right man, and that man could never be Mark Rowlands.

'Ghostly, isn't it?' she said aloud.

'Ghostly?' echoed a voice not far from her ear.

'The flickering light, the shadows...'

'Scared, Tiffany?' Mark asked drily.

'No...'

'Want to go back to the car?'

'Oh, no!' She turned to him quickly. 'I want to see the house.'

'For a moment you had me wondering.'

'Mark...' He was walking once more, when she touched his arm and felt the flexing of hard muscles beneath her fingertips. 'You have to know, I was heartbroken when Andrew died. I knew about the inheritance, but it didn't mean anything to me—not then, anyway.'

Torchlight played on Tiffany's face. 'Why are you telling me this now? At this particular moment?'

Mark's face was behind the light, making it impossible for Tiffany to see his eyes, but she did not doubt that their expression would be cynical.

'Because I want you to know the way it was,' she said slowly. 'It was a while before I thought about all the things Andrew had left me. When I did, my first idea was to instruct you to sell the house. Think of it . . . a property thousands of miles away, on another continent . . . I was never likely to have any use for it. I wrote you a letter, I was on the point of posting it, and then I thought—why not just take a look at the place?'

'And now you're here.' Mark's tone was laconic.

'Now I'm here. I never imagined I'd have my first sight of the house at night, by torchlight. I'll probably always remember it this way. A house of shadows. Of shapes. A house of ghosts, all waiting to welcome me.'

'I believe you have a romantic soul, rose nymph.'

'Who? Me?' She remembered her own earlier thought, and danced him a look which she doubted he could see in the dim light. 'I'm a dreadful person, a schemer—remember?'

'Not at this moment,' he said softly. 'We agreed that tonight was for make-believe.'

As tomorrow would be once more for accusations. Tiffany had no illusions that Mark Rowlands—tough, ruthless and intimidating—would let the mood of this evening carry over into his handling of Andrew's estate.

'There is no such thing as make-believe,' she said flatly.

'You don't really mean that,' he answered, and propelled her further.

Even in the darkness, Tiffany grasped the fact that the house had none of the cosiness of the cottage she had shared with Andrew. There was only sparseness and size.

'It needs changes,' she said thoughtfully.

'You won't be here long enough to make any.' Mark's tone was harsh.

Tiffany turned to him. 'You'd like me to stay here just long enough to instruct you to sell the house. And then you'd very happily see me on the next plane, wouldn't you, Mark?'

'Have I said that?'

'You haven't had to. I know you can't wait to see the back of me.'

'Don't mind-read, Tiffany,' Mark said tautly.

She decided to stand her ground. 'Why not? It isn't difficult, you know. You've made no secret of your feelings.'

Once more they stood together in a silence that was too tense, too charged.

At last Mark said, 'We're here—you may as well see the rest of it.'

Tiffany followed the slender beam of the torch into a dining-room, where all she could make out was a long table with chairs around it, then into a large kitchen, and cool stone-floored bathrooms. At the end of the passage were the bedrooms.

'This,' Mark said, throwing open the last door, 'is the master bedroom. Andrew's parents slept here.'

Tiffany watched the torchlight play over the walls. 'Andrew used to talk about his parents. What a big room this is, Mark.'

'Big enough for a double bed.'

She heard the edge in his tone, and caught the innuendo. 'If this were my home, I'd have no need for a double bed,' she countered with deliberate lightness.

'You might want a replacement for Andrew.'

Tiffany grew rigid. 'We had an agreement. Not another word tonight about my relationship with Andrew.'

'Actually,' Mark said insolently, 'the condition was that I wouldn't mention him in the restaurant.'

'You're twisting my words. Is that the lawyer in you?' Tiffany asked coldly. She paused a moment, then went on more quietly, 'You still don't believe that I was never Andrew's mistress.'

'You've admitted you loved him.'

'I did, very much. Platonically.'

'If not Andrew—then who is the man in your life?'

'There isn't one.'

'No?' A hard edge of cynicism in his tone.

'No,' Tiffany said firmly.

'Why not?'

'I don't want a man. I don't need one.'

'I don't believe you,' he said, as he reached for her and drew her into his arms.

He moved so quickly that Tiffany did not have a chance to get away from him. By the time she knew what was happening, Mark was holding her tightly and his mouth was on hers. Outraged, she closed her lips firmly and pushed at him with balled hands. But Mark laughed against her mouth, and kissed her harder. Tiffany's sense of outrage increased, but only briefly, as her anger gave way to a more powerful emotion. Mark's kisses grew more and more passionate, and a fire began to smoulder in Tiffany's veins.

The torch dropped to the floor, and Tiffany and Mark stood together in the darkness, so close that it seemed to Tiffany as if every inch of the long male body was welded to hers. She was barely thinking when her arms reached around Mark's neck and she opened her lips to him.

Later, she could not have said how long their kisses lasted, but when they drew apart she felt weak. She was glad of the darkness in the room, and the private moment in which to regain her composure.

She turned away from Mark as he bent to retrieve the torch.

'You shouldn't have done that,' she said jerkily, when she could speak once more.

'Kissed you?' Light played on her face. 'You enjoyed it as much as I did. Admit it, Tiffany.'

She *had* enjoyed it. Far too much. And she would die rather than tell him so.

Lifting her head, she made herself meet his gaze. 'Why did you do it?'

'Why does a man kiss a woman?' He sounded amused.

'To prove something?'

'You could say I wanted a question answered.'

His tone was mild, but in the dim light Tiffany saw the intensity of his gaze.

'Mark...' Suddenly, she was trembling.

'There's passion in you, rose nymph.'

'A few kisses don't prove a thing,' she said unsteadily.

'They prove that a platonic friendship has no place in your life. But you've known that all along, haven't you, Tiffany?'

'Don't!' she burst out angrily. 'No more questions about my love-life!'

She turned her head so that he would not see the tears that had sprung unexpectedly to her eyes. She shivered as she heard his low laugh.

'No more questions,' he drawled. 'I already have the answer I need.'

CHAPTER THREE

THE front-desk receptionist looked amazed when Tiffany asked her for directions to Andrew's house. But she spent a few minutes consulting a map, and in no time at all Tiffany was in possession of a neatly drawn sketch with intersections, traffic lights and roads all clearly marked.

The next step was to rent a car, a little vehicle that was so like the one Tiffany was accustomed to that she was comfortable with it right away. The receptionist's directions were easy to follow, and it was not long before Tiffany had left the city behind her.

There was so little traffic on the road that she was able to observe the countryside as she drove. In the darkness of the previous night, she had been aware of vastness and isolation, but now she was fascinated with great stretches of land unimpeded by walls and hedges, land that was covered with trees which she recognised from the pictures Andrew had shown her: bluegums and maroelas and umbrella-shaped acacias.

Once, in a stretch of windswept *veld*, she stopped the car to marvel at the strangest-looking tree she had ever seen. Its girth was colossal, its branches so disproportionately tiny, that a smiling Tiffany was reminded of a giant who'd had his hair cropped far too short. Andrew had shown her pictures of baobabs. An elephant could shelter in a baobab's trunk, he had said, and Tiffany had been certain he was teasing. Now she thought he might have stretched the truth—but not by much.

She stopped again to look at a rock formation, one bare rock balanced on another in an unlikely acrobatic feat of nature. Rocks that looked as if they would come tumbling down if you so much as touched them. Andrew had told her about the rocks too.

But the rocks and the baobabs had adorned the hot, dry land for centuries, and Tiffany had things to do. She drove further, glad of the air-conditioning in the car, eager to reach the house before the heat grew even more intense.

She had been driving close to an hour when she came to a sign that she recognised, and then she was turning off the highway and on to a dusty road.

Reaching the house, she turned off the engine, but she did not get out of the car right away. Sitting forward in her seat, she gazed through the windscreen.

How different the house looked in the daytime. The roof was red, as was the window-trim. On one side was a long veranda, and surrounding the house on three sides were the tall bluegums Tiffany had seen elsewhere. The remains of a lawn sloped away from the house, but the rough grass was brown and dry, testimony to the vicious drought that had so much of Africa in its grip.

But there was colour here too. A scarlet bougainvillaea cascaded over the trellis of the veranda, and a hibiscus trumpeted its great yellow flowers near the front door—tropical shrubs which proclaimed their ability to survive even when water was scarce.

This was the house where Andrew had spent his boyhood years. The garden he had played in. The trees he had climbed. And beyond it, the *veld* where he had ridden his first horse.

Andrew's house. Her house now...

The previous evening, Tiffany and Mark had returned to the city in silence. Tiffany, in a turmoil of emotion which she did not care to identify, had been in no mood for conversation. Somewhat surprisingly, Mark had made no attempt to talk either.

They were outside the hotel when Tiffany had turned to Mark and asked him for the keys.

'To the house?'

'Yes.'

'Planning to go there alone?'

'I might.'

With the door open, the ceiling light illuminated the car, and Tiffany was able to see Mark's face. His deep long-lashed eyes were shuttered, the sensuous lips unsmiling, his expression dark and smouldering.

'I understand the house isn't legally mine yet,' Tiffany had said quietly, 'but you can't object to me spending some time there on my own?'

A searching look. And then a careless shrug as Mark reached into his pocket for the keys. Tiffany took them from him, tensing as his fingers closed, just for a moment, around hers. When he released her hand, her fingers burned where he had touched them.

'It's your house,' he said curtly. 'Naturally, you're entitled to go there whenever you please.'

Tiffany nodded as their eyes locked for a long moment. There was no prolonged goodbye. Seconds after Tiffany had closed the door of the car, it had vanished in the darkness.

And she *would* come here whenever she pleased, Tiffany told herself now. Making an effort to push away the picture of Mark's face which, after just one day's acquaintance, had an annoying way of inserting itself into her mind, she left the car and walked towards the house.

Strangely, she felt a little like an intruder as she put the key in the lock and walked inside. For a few minutes she stood motionless in the entrance hall, and listened to the silence. Then she began to retrace the path she had taken with Mark.

Without the cloak of darkness, the house lacked the mystery of the previous night. Yesterday Tiffany had been aware only of spaciousness, today she saw shabbiness as well. A pervasive shabbiness, legacy of a procession of tenants with no interest or pride in the property.

The walls were in need of fresh paint. The furniture—the little that was worth keeping—needed to be polished and cleaned. Curtains and carpets were mostly threadbare. Yet the shabbiness was not as depressing as it might have been, for the gracefully proportioned house had potential. It had been lovely once, Tiffany thought. With some care and attention it could be lovely again.

Slowly she wandered from one room to another, working her way from the front of the house to the back. In the doorway of the master bedroom she paused. Her eyes moved downwards, pausing at scuffmarks in the dust, marks left by two pairs of shoes, a woman's and a man's, close together. The spot where Tiffany and Mark had kissed. Tiffany shivered as she relived the passion of Mark's embrace and the uninhibited nature of her own response. Lips tight, she closed the door of the room with a bang.

Leaving the house by the back door, she saw that the property was even bigger than she had realised. Several acres, at least. Someone had made an attempt at cultivating a vegetable garden, and fruit trees dotted the dry ground. In the distance stood a barn.

A huge barn, Tiffany saw, as she walked towards it. In the open doorway, a familiar smell greeted her. A faint smell, but one that Tiffany knew and loved—the smell of horses.

Interested now, she looked around her. It had been some time, she thought, since there'd been any horses here, but in the dimness she saw bits of old straw and hay littering the ground. And then her eyes caught something else, an object so covered with straw that she almost missed it. An old saddle. Tiffany could not have said why she picked it up and carried it outside.

In the sunlight, she looked at it closely. The saddle was very dusty, the leather cracked with age. Tiffany rubbed at it with her fingers, her interest quickening when letters, scratched into the leather, began to show through the dust. More rubbing, and the letters took shape. And then a name appeared. ANDREW. D and R turned the wrong way, E barely legible. The letters were achingly familiar. The awkward writing of a dyslexic who had never been taught how to overcome his disability.

Closing her eyes, Tiffany leaned back against the sun-warmed wall of the barn. Andrew had taken her into his home shortly after the break-up with Wayde. Her parents had died in a motor accident a few years earlier, and there had been nobody else for her to turn to. Because she understood horses, Andrew had taken her on as an employee. Within a short time they had become fast friends.

It had been a while before Tiffany had understood why Andrew never wrote a letter, never signed a cheque, relied on television rather than on reading for news. When she did, she went to the library and searched for books about dyslexia, then sent for an instructional course with information on how to help a person overcome the problem. During the day she worked with Andrew in the stables, taking care of the horses and teaching children how to ride. At night they sat together before the living-room fire, and slowly, lovingly, patiently, Tiffany tried to teach Andrew how to read and write.

Holding Andrew's saddle against her chest, inhaling the smell of ancient leather, Tiffany blinked back tears of sorrow. She knew that she would never stop missing the man who had been her best friend.

When the tears had dried, her eyes went once more to the house that had been Andrew's home. An unexpected idea was beginning to take shape in her mind.

* * *

An hour later Tiffany was in Mark's office and telling his receptionist that she wanted to see him.

The girl looked at her doubtfully. 'Do you have an appointment, Miss Marlow?'

'No...'

'Mr Rowlands is busy.'

'I'd really like to see him. It's very important. Is there a time today when he'll be free?'

'I'll find out.'

As the receptionist walked down the long passage, high heels clicking on the polished wooden floor, Tiffany went to stand at the big plate-glass windows that surrounded the office on three sides. From the ninth floor there was a panoramic view of the city office towers and distant suburbs yielding to a vista of bush that extended all the way to the horizon. Somewhere in that bush was a red-roofed farmhouse where a man had spent the most impressionable years of his life. Though the house was empty and dilapidated now, the man's last will had made it possible for it to come alive once more.

Had that been Andrew's last wish?

'Miss Marlow...?'

Tiffany turned. Lost in thought, she had not heard the receptionist return.

'Mr Rowlands will see you now.' The girl was regarding Tiffany curiously, perhaps because it was unusual for a busy lawyer to see anyone at such short notice. 'Down the passage, third door on the right.'

'I remember.' Tiffany gave the receptionist a grateful smile. 'And thank you.'

She stopped when she came to the door with the neat brass plate. So much hinged on this meeting, and she felt a little nervous suddenly. But she gave herself a mental shake, squared her shoulders, and knocked.

The door opened, and there was Mark, his broad-shouldered body filling the doorway. The formal Mark Rowlands, the lawyer in the expensive grey suit.

'Hello, Tiffany,' he said, and his grin made him once more the man who had kissed her in the dark farmhouse.

Tiffany tried to ignore her heartbeat, an insistent tattoo against her ribs. 'Hello, Mark. Thanks for agreeing to see me so quickly.'

Mark moved aside, and Tiffany walked into the room, stopping short at sight of a woman standing near the desk. A woman in her late twenties, an exquisite cream-coloured suit revealing her superb figure. She wore pearls at her neck and ears, and her shining blonde hair was swept back in a chignon that accentuated her classic features. Well-groomed and quite beautiful, she could have been a fashion model.

'I'm sorry...' Feeling a little inadequate in her own much simpler clothes, Tiffany looked at Mark in confusion. 'I understood that you were free. I...I didn't realise I was intruding...'

'I told Ann to send you in.' Mark glanced at the woman, then back at Tiffany. 'Actually, we had just finished our business. Clarissa, I want you to meet Tiffany Marlow. Tiffany—this is Clarissa Donaldson.'

Her momentary sense of uncertainty forgotten, Tiffany quickly closed the gap between herself and the other woman, and held out her hand. 'I'm so glad to meet you.'

Clarissa's hand-shake was cool and brief, but in the excitement of the moment, Tiffany made nothing of it.

'You must be related to Andrew,' she said eagerly.

A slight nod. 'Our fathers were brothers.'

'Billy's daughter?'

Clarissa shrugged. 'My father's name was William.'

'William... I guess Andrew still thought of him as Billy. Fifteen years separated them, you know, and Andrew had left home long before B...William grew up. Andrew was very upset when your father died. I think he wished he'd got to know him a little better.'

'Is that so?' Not a flicker of expression crossed the beautiful face.

'Could we get together, Miss Donaldson? I've just arrived from England—yesterday, actually, as Mark might have told you. Are you free this week by any chance? I'd love to meet you for lunch.'

Clarissa gave Mark a quick look before turning back to Tiffany. 'Sorry, but I'm not free this week.'

'Some other time then? And I want to meet the rest of Andrew's family as well.'

Cold eyes swept Tiffany's face. 'I won't be free at all, Miss Marlow. And I hardly think I'm talking out of turn when I tell you that the rest of the family won't be free either.'

Tiffany felt as if she had been slapped, very hard, across the face. She took an involuntary step backwards.

But Clarissa seemed not to have noticed the consequences of her rudeness. She was looking at Mark once more. 'You will phone me, darling?'

Darling? Tiffany wondered numbly.

'When I have news for you about the sale,' said Mark, who had remained silent throughout the brief exchange.

'I hope that will be very soon. You know how anxious I am to get the whole thing finalised.' The blonde put her hand on Mark's arm and said, ''Bye, darling,' before kissing him firmly on the lips. Barely looking at Tiffany, she added, 'Goodbye, Miss Marlow.'

When Clarissa Donaldson was gone, Tiffany challenged Mark. 'Why did you subject me to that?' Her cheeks were flaming. 'Couldn't you have waited until she'd gone before letting me see you? What are you, Mark Rowlands—a sadist? Does it give you pleasure to see me humiliated?'

'Is that what you believe?' His eyes were without expression.

'I don't know what to believe any more,' Tiffany said flatly. 'Clarissa called you darling; you must know her very well. Didn't you guess she'd be rude?'

She waited a moment, but Mark did not respond.

After a few seconds, Tiffany went on, 'I believe you knew precisely the reception I was in for. It was unforgivable of you to put me through it, Mark.'

'Don't be so dramatic, Tiffany. Clarissa was here, so were you—I decided to introduce you.'

'And that's all there was to it? I was so happy to hear the name Donaldson. You heard me inviting that...that *barracuda* to have lunch with me. Will the rest of the family dislike me too? How can they, when we haven't even met?'

Hooded eyes studied Tiffany's hot face. 'I've told you how Andrew's relatives feel about his will.'

Tiffany's head jerked up. 'It doesn't make sense!' She threw the words at him. 'Yes, I know we went over this yesterday, but Andrew's wife and child had died. Even Clarissa's father, Andrew's only immediate relative, is no longer alive. As for the rest of them, none of them was close family. And there'd been so little contact. Was he obliged to remember them in his will?'

'You tell me, Tiffany.'

'Andrew was his own man, Mark. He did as he liked.'

'*That's* what doesn't make sense to me. I keep going back to it. If Andrew was really his own man, why did he leave the running of his personal affairs to someone else?'

Tiffany stared at Mark. How easy it would be to tell him the truth—and how impossible.

'It was the way he wanted it,' she said simply.

'An employee. Entrusted with so much responsibility.' Mark's voice was laced with cynicism.

'Employee and *friend*,' Tiffany corrected him sharply. 'We've been over this too.'

'We have, haven't we?'

She heard the mockery in his tone. Involuntarily, her mind went back to the previous evening. Mark had talked of make-believe and adults playing games. His magic had got to her, allowing her, despite her better judgement, to believe that a respite was possible. Perhaps she had even hoped that a few pleasant hours together could change the way he thought about her. *Stupid*! she reproached herself now.

They were still standing. Dark eyes held green ones, defying them to look away. Mark put his hands on Tiffany's shoulders, and she felt a little weak. He was too big, too dangerous, too dominating.

'I think I should go,' she said unsteadily.

'Ann said you had to see me.' His hands tightened on her shoulders.

'It can wait...'

'She seemed to think it was important.'

'Well, yes...'

He loosened his hands. 'Sit down.'

'Another time,' Tiffany muttered.

'Now.' It was an order that could not be refused.

Mark sat down at his desk. A little shaken, Tiffany took the chair she had sat in a day earlier.

'Why did you want to see me, Tiffany?'

She took a breath. 'Money.'

'So that's it.' His tone was steel-hard.

Tiffany's head lifted. 'Will it always be like this between us, Mark?'

'Perhaps.'

'How many lawyers are there in Bulawayo?'

'Enough.'

'And you're the one I had to be saddled with. Are you quite sure I can't find another trustee?'

A dark eyebrow lifted in a taunt. 'Quite.'

Tiffany regarded him bitterly. 'I don't see how we'll ever be able to get on together if you're always going to be so arrogant.'

He grinned at her in a way that was becoming familiar. 'We've been over this too. How much do you want, Tiffany?'

She hesitated a moment. 'Quite a lot,' she said then.

'Enough to pay your hotel bills and the rental of the car you drove out to the house?'

'So you know about the car.'

'There are things I know, Tiffany. Getting back to the money, how much do you want?'

She gave it to him squarely. 'A few thousand.'

For a moment Mark looked stunned. Then he sat forward in his chair. 'How many thousand?'

'Three, maybe more. For a start.'

A dangerous glint appeared in Mark's eyes. 'So,' he said thinly, 'the ingenuous little rose nymph was never more than a gold-digger after all. Despite all her protests to the contrary.'

'*How dare you*?' She flung the words at him furiously.

'The facts speak for themselves.'

'I'm entitled to the money, Mark.'

'Only if you satisfy me that you need it.'

'You obviously think that I don't.'

'What I think is,' he said pointedly, 'that my first assessment of you was correct all along. You were always after Andrew's money.'

'*No*!'

But he went on as if he had not heard her anguished protest. 'You played your cards well when you got Andrew to leave you everything he owned.' He paused a moment. 'Not quite well enough, of course—we talked about that yesterday. You'd have come up trumps if he'd left you the inheritance outright. I'd give much to know why he was happier leaving the money in trust. Not that it matters, since you can't get your little hands on it automatically.'

Tiffany shot out of her chair. 'I've heard enough!'

She was at the door when a quiet voice called her back. 'Why do you want the money?'

She ignored the question. Slamming the door behind her, she ran out of the office.

Three messages were waiting for Tiffany when she returned to the hotel later in the day. She had no intention of reading them. When she was out of sight of the front desk, she crumpled the three bits of paper into a tight ball and shoved them into the nearest rubbish bin.

The phone rang soon after she reached her room, the sound jarring in the hot stillness. She let it ring, and eventually it stopped. It rang again twice after that, and both times Tiffany ignored it. Only one person in Bulawayo would be phoning her, and she did not want to speak to him.

She ordered her dinner from room service, forcing herself to choose a dish from a menu which did not appeal to her any more than on the previous day. In the event, she barely touched the meal. When the tray had been collected, she went to the window and looked outside.

It was dark by now. Cars raced through the streets of Bulawayo, and from a nearby restaurant came the blare of pop music. Last night, at Andrew's house, the singing of the crickets had filled the air. Today, a dream had been born there. But Mark Rowlands was the master of Tiffany's destiny, at least as far as her inheritance was concerned, and so that dream could not be realised. Which meant that there was nothing for her in Zimbabwe. Tomorrow she would consult a travel agent about a flight back to England.

Tiffany was about to shower the next morning when there was a knock at her door. With some surprise, she glanced at her watch, and realised that room service was half an hour early with her breakfast.

She opened the door and said, 'It's a bit soon——' And then, '*Mark*!'

'Hello, rose nymph.'

Looking at the vibrant man in the denim shorts and figure-hugging navy sports shirt, Tiffany was swept with a pleasure that sent the blood racing through her veins. It was a few seconds before she remembered that Mark was her enemy.

She tried to close the door. But he was faster than she was, his foot inserting itself between the door and the frame.

His laughter was deep-throated and amused. 'Not the best way to get rid of me, Tiffany.'

'You weren't invited!'

'You could have answered my messages. Or the phone. I happen to know you were here when I rang.'

'Did it occur to you that I might not want to speak to you?'

'Even though you knew that *I* wanted to speak to *you*?'

'So that you could accuse me of more of the same? I'm sick of hearing what an awful person I am. Are you going to remove your beastly foot from the door, Mark Rowlands, or do I have to call security to remove it for you?'

'It's up to you, Tiffany. Just remember, if you have me booted out, I may never know why you wanted the money.'

Tiffany hesitated a moment. 'Does it matter? You've already turned down my request.'

'Actually, I haven't.'

'A greedy gold-digger—that's how you think of me.'

'You walked out while I was asking you for details.'

'Are you saying you're curious?'

'Are you going to let me in, Tiffany?'

Again she hesitated. Her first instinct had been the right one, she thought—call security, and let them deal with this obnoxious hot-shot lawyer. She could still do it.

'What do you have to lose?' he asked softly.

There was her pride, but that did not seem to matter much. And then there was her heart, the condition of which was already treacherously precarious.

Something in his manner persuaded her. 'All right,' she said, and stepped away from the door.

He walked inside, big, tanned, his presence immediately robbing the hotel room of its sterility. His eyes travelled over Tiffany's body, and something stirred inside her. She was learning that desire could spring to life quickly, that it could heat the blood within seconds.

'You're quite a sight, rose nymph,' Mark said softly.

Until that moment, Tiffany had forgotten that she was wearing shortie pyjamas, diaphanous bits of red trimmed with black lace, which she had bought on a whim. She moved restlessly under the probing male gaze.

'You know very well that I wasn't expecting you.'

'Yet you opened the door at the first knock. Obviously you're used to receiving people in such sexy attire.'

'I thought you were room service with my breakfast.'

An eyebrow arched provocatively. 'You were going to let a waiter see you like this?'

'They have waitresses here.' Tiffany lifted her chin at him. 'Besides, I wasn't expecting my breakfast yet. I was about to shower, and I don't know what the hell you're insinuating anyway.'

'Don't you?' he drawled.

'You may be my trustee, Mark Rowlands, but that's the limit of our association. If I choose to walk through the streets of the city naked, it would be none of your business.'

'If that's what you're planning to do, Tiffany, I'd appreciate advance warning. It would be a sight I'd hate to miss.'

Caught by his husky laughter, Tiffany looked up at him, at the deep-set eyes, the sensuous lips and tanned throat, and she felt her heart thud hard in her chest. Arrogant he might be, yet Tiffany was well aware that she had never met a more dynamic man than Mark Rowlands.

'Better still,' he suggested, 'why don't you let me appreciate your nakedness in private?'

'I think you should go, Mark,' she said through dry lips.

'You were about to shower.'

'When you've gone...'

'Let's shower together.'

'Don't be ridiculous!'

'Is it ridiculous, rose nymph?'

Her heart was beating so hard now that she was sure he must hear it. 'It's more than ridiculous,' she told him with all the firmness she could muster. 'It's outrageous!'

'But so very tempting.'

'No,' she whispered, wishing she meant it.

'You don't sound at all convincing.'

He came towards her, and she moved away, only to find the wall at her back. And then he had closed the distance between them and was drawing her to him. A moment later his mouth had descended and his lips were brushing hers, lightly, tantalisingly, so erotically that her hunger increased.

As if he sensed her emotion, his kisses became more passionate. His tongue pushed at her lips and his teeth bit her lightly. Tiffany gasped. And then she opened her mouth to him, and her hands went around his neck, her fingers burying themselves in the thick dark hair at his collar. He was holding her very tightly now, his long body hard and strong against hers, and the hunger inside her became an ache, quite unlike anything she had ever experienced, even with Wayde.

Mark pushed the flimsy pyjama-top from Tiffany's shoulders. And then his lips descended further, brushing first her throat, and then the soft swell above her breasts, teasing her breasts with his tongue—and all the while Tiffany's heart was like a captive bird, beating its wings against the walls of its cage.

She was almost beyond rational thought when Mark lifted his head. 'Someone's knocking.'

'Knocking...?' Tiffany repeated, dazed.

The sound came again, and she moved out of Mark's arms as he said, 'Your breakfast?'

'I think so...' She looked down at herself, her cheeks flaming as she saw her near-naked state. 'My God, Mark... I can't let anyone see me like this! What am I going to do?'

'I'll look after it,' he said.

Tiffany sank back against the wall, out of sight of the door. Mark took the tray and thanked the waitress. By the time he turned back to Tiffany, she had pulled on her pyjama-top once more.

'What did the waitress say?' she asked faintly.

'Enjoy your breakfast, sir.'

'*Sir*. Breakfast for one, and the name on the tray is Miss Marlow.'

Dark eyes sparkled. 'Bothers you, does it?'

'I'm wondering what she thought.'

'Nothing more taxing than that you were enjoying a spot of pre-breakfast fun.'

'You are so slick, Mark.' She looked at him bitterly.

Putting down the tray, he came towards her. 'Why should the truth offend you, Tiffany? You were enjoying yourself.'

Unable to deny the obvious, she shrank from him, arms folded across her chest. 'It doesn't matter now anyway. It's over.'

'Because we were disturbed?'

'Because I wasn't thinking,' she said unhappily. 'It shouldn't have happened.'

'I'm glad it did. We can still shower together, Tiffany.'

'Please go, Mark.'

'You don't really mean that.'

'I do.'

He came towards her, his arms going around her, trying to draw her to him once more, but she made herself stiff.

With a firmness that surprised her, she said, 'Go, Mark.'

His arms dropped, and Tiffany felt bereft.

He was at the door when he turned. 'We're forgetting why I'm here. You left my office yesterday without telling me why you wanted so much money.'

Dully, Tiffany said, 'It's no longer important.'

'Why not?'

'Because you'll never let me have it. You're so certain I manipulated Andrew, you don't believe I deserve that money.'

'Prove me wrong,' he said quietly. 'Tell me why you need it. I want to know.'

Looking at him, Tiffany saw that he was serious. 'I had a dream.' Tears stung her eyelids. She turned her head away; she did not want Mark to have the satisfaction of seeing her cry.

'A dream, Tiffany?' His hand cupped her chin, forcing her to look at him.

'Well?' he prompted.

'Stables,' she said in a low voice.

'*Stables*?' he repeated incredulously.

'I thought of living here, of making Andrew's house my home. Doing in Zimbabwe the things Andrew and I did together in England.'

'Well,' Mark said again, but this time the word indicated interest rather than a question. 'Tell me more about this dream.'

'Now?' she asked uncertainly, wondering whether she could trust this abrupt change of heart. 'Here?'

'Not a good idea,' he replied drily. 'You're a very sexy woman, rose nymph, and I'm too warm-blooded a male not to want to make love to you.'

She began to tremble. 'Mark...'

His eyes held hers for a long moment, as if he guessed at the turbulence of her emotions.

'We'll drive out to the house,' he said then. '*Your* house, Tiffany. We'll take a picnic, and you can show me what you have in mind.'

'It's a weekday, Mark.'

'That's right.'

'Now that I think of it, what are you doing here anyway? Shouldn't you be wearing a suit, doing important things in your office?'

'I decided to take the day off.'

'Why did you do that?'

'Isn't it enough that I did? I'll take care of the food while you get dressed. I'll meet you back here in half an hour.'

Spoken with such superb confidence. As if it never occurred to Mark that anyone might not want to do as he said.

'Wait for me in the foyer,' Tiffany said, a little too quickly.

She forced herself to smile as he left the room. But as the door closed behind him, she wondered if he knew that more than anything else she had wanted to go back into his arms and let him make love to her.

CHAPTER FOUR

'FINISH all that breakfast?' Mark asked, when he'd spread a rug in the shade of a dusty bluegum.

Green eyes sparkled at him. 'Showered, dressed and eaten in twenty minutes? I may be fast, Mark Rowlands, but not that fast. I'll have you know that I left the tray outside the door, untouched.'

'Just as well,' he answered with a wicked grin.

The sun shone on his face, emphasising the strongly chiselled features and highlighting the flecks of gold in his eyes. Tiffany had tried telling herself that she had magnified him in her imagination, that no man could possibly live up to her mental picture of him. Yet the reality was that Mark seemed more attractive every time they met, his intelligence and humour combining with a tough sexiness that seemed to make him irresistible.

With an effort she tore her gaze from his face and focused on the basket which he had put on the ground beside the rug. Fascinated, she watched as he unpacked its contents: a crusty loaf of French bread, a slab of yellow cheese, fat green olives, two golden mangoes and a bottle of wine.

'Regretting your breakfast after all?' Mark teased, as she knelt on the rug.

'Coffee and two sad-looking scones can't begin to compare with this feast. I admit to being impressed. You managed all this in twenty minutes? You've brought enough food for a week.'

'Maybe we should consider camping out here, in that case. How about it, Tiffany?'

She knew he was teasing, yet the thought was infinitely exciting all the same. 'Do people actually camp in the wilds of Africa?' she asked him.

'Naturally, but you're hardly in the wilds, Tiffany—there's a sophisticated city not an hour away.'

'Are there no animals in the bush?'

'Nothing too spectacular. Baboons, the odd leopard.'

'Snakes?' she asked doubtfully.

'Those too.' He laughed as she shivered. 'I'd make a fire and nothing menacing would venture near us.'

'Absolutely not, Mark. The very thought of a snake would be enough to keep me awake all night.'

'We could stay awake together. Think what fun we'd have while I protected you.'

Something in the way he said the words made Tiffany catch her breath. Their eyes held for an interminable moment, and then Mark's eyes moved downwards, going quite deliberately to Tiffany's lips.

She had not realised quite how near he was to her. She could see every muscle in his arms and legs and the dark hair that curled on his chest.

'You'd feel safe with me, wouldn't you, Tiffany?' he asked very softly.

Could there be any safety with a man who would play havoc with her emotions? Unscrupulously so, because he deemed her unscrupulous too, and therefore not deserving of consideration or respect.

'Should I feel safe?' she asked, not quite steadily.

'I protected you from the vengeance of the cyclist.'

'That was different.'

'Of course,' he drawled suggestively, 'if you're not comfortable outside, we could always camp indoors instead. I'd spread the rug on the living-room floor. If it was cold in the night I'd chop a few logs and make a fire in the fireplace, and we could watch the flames and pretend we were in the bush.'

'More adult games...'

His eyes glinted. 'More games,' he agreed.

And when the flames began to die he would try to make love to her, and that streak of passion which had surprised her earlier today would get the better of her, and she would be unable to resist him.

'Well, Tiffany?'

She made an attempt at a merry smile. 'I think I prefer the comfort of my hotel room.'

Mark laughed again, the sound infinitely seductive on the silent air. 'And I think you're tempted but frightened.'

'I don't know about you,' Tiffany said brightly, 'but the sight of all that delicious food is making me hungry.'

Dark eyes glinted. 'All right, Tiffany, we'll change the subject if it's getting too hot for you. For now, anyway. Will you cut the bread and the cheese while I open the wine?'

For the next few minutes Tiffany made herself very busy with the food while Mark uncorked the bottle and poured the wine. They helped themselves to bread and cheese and olives, and Tiffany took a sip of her wine.

They had almost finished their meal when Mark reached out and tugged at the hair which Tiffany had caught backwards in an elastic band. 'Today you're a tomboy.'

It was Tiffany's turn to laugh. 'For years I was just that. I didn't own a dress until I was sixteen. All the things I enjoyed most were best done in trousers—running, climbing trees, riding my horse along the beach.'

'Interesting,' Mark mused, 'because to me you're all female. You're a woman of mystery, rose nymph. Just when I think I know you, I find I don't know you after all.'

She danced him a provocative look. 'Woman of mystery—I like that.'

'I like it too.'

She thought he was teasing again until she saw the naked look in his eyes, the hint of something shocking and a little primitive. And suddenly Tiffany was wishing with all her heart that she could have met this man in a different time, a different place. Wishing too that Andrew had not made her give a promise which, she sensed, would become more and more difficult to keep.

A little wildly, she cast about in her mind for some way to change the subject once more. She remembered the reason they had come here today, but until now there had been no mention of the stables. It was time to talk about them now, before she got into waters which might well be too deep for her.

With a briskness she was far from feeling, she said, 'The picnic was delicious, Mark, but that's not why we're here. I'd like to hear your thoughts.'

'Remember that you asked for this, Tiffany.' His eyes moved over her body in a way that unnerved her. 'My thoughts are that I want you. I want to go on where we stopped earlier. I want to undress you, I want to kiss every inch of your sexy body, I want to make mad, frantic, passionate love to you out here on the grass. And then——'

'*Don't!*' she whispered in a strangled voice.

'Afraid we'll be seen? I assure you there's nobody for miles around. But if you're really shy, Tiffany, we could go indoors, spread the rug, and——'

A shiver of desire ran through her, sharp as an electric current, but she knew she had to divert him. 'The stables,' she said unsteadily.

'Why bring them up now?'

She understood that he was baiting her, that his look of amazement was nothing but pretence.

'You knew exactly what I meant when I asked you your thoughts,' she persevered hardily. 'My stables... They're the reason we're here today.' His lips tilted in a cynical smile, and she made herself go on calmly despite the heat that stained her cheeks. 'The *only* reason, Mark. I wish you'd stop taunting me. Do I get the money, or don't I?'

Mark raised himself on one elbow. 'Business it is, then. Tell me what you have in mind.'

Tiffany sat up straight. A tease and a flirt Mark Rowlands might be, but he was also a man with diverse responsibilities, and she sensed that where money was involved only a reasoned approach would impress him. When she went on talking she made her voice calm, cool and professional.

'I understand horses, Mark. I've already told you something about my work with Andrew. You know that we gave lessons and that people boarded their animals in our stables.'

'And you're thinking of doing those things here.'

'Yes.' Anxiously she searched eyes that had become hooded, and wished she could tell what Mark was thinking.

'You're talking of a big undertaking, Tiffany.'

'I could make a success of it.'

'You're a long way from home.'

'I know that.'

'You might be very lonely out here in the bush.'

'I'd be so busy, the lack of people wouldn't bother me.'

'We have problems with drought.'

'I know that too. I've seen the dry grass, the empty ponds and streams.'

'They don't scare you?'

'A little, but not enough to put me off. People do go on living in Africa. There must be farmers with livestock, ranchers with horses.'

'Do you have any idea what you'd be getting yourself into, Tiffany?'

'I think I do. I'm not stupid.'

'I never thought you were.'

'But you think I use my mind only to scheme and manipulate.' Tiffany paused a moment, giving Mark a chance to deny the statement. When he did not, she lifted her head angrily. 'I may never be able to change your mind about me, and perhaps that doesn't matter. The fact is, my plans don't involve anyone but myself. I mean to start my own stables here, Mark.'

'But you can't—unless I give you the OK.' His eyes were narrow now; he was watching her carefully. Nothing left of the incorrigible flirt: he was all shrewd lawyer now.

'It's *my* money, Mark.'

'Of which I happen to be the trustee.'

'I don't need reminding.' She looked at him unhappily.

Mark was silent as he looked into the distance, his gaze seeming to go across the fields and the windswept *veld* to the horizon. Tiffany grew tense as she watched him.

It was a while before he turned back to her. 'It doesn't make sense to me. If it's stables you want, Tiffany, you have them already—in England. You're Andrew's sole beneficiary there as well; you've inherited everything he owned. Why don't you just carry on with what you have?'

'Because I want to try something new. This is my land, Mark, and I want to use it. Is that so difficult to understand?'

'It is for me. I believe you'd soon start hankering after England. I believe it would be a darn sight easier for you there, in the country you know so well.'

Tiffany was conscious of a sharp sense of disappointment. Letting her gaze go to a lizard that was slithering over a sun-warmed rock, she pretended an interest in the small reptilian creature. Mark had no interest in her, that much seemed clear. Whether she returned to England or stayed in Zimbabwe was a matter of sheer indifference to him. If anything, his last words seemed to indicate that he would be happy to see her leave.

How could she have let herself believe, even for a moment, that he was anything but a flirt? she asked herself angrily. A man who probably looked upon every woman as a potential conquest, who moved from one female to another as easily as a bee darting between flowers. Who did not care if a woman was hurt when he toyed with her emotions. She kept her eyes fixed on the agile lizard, determined that her expression would not reveal her feelings.

'Tiffany?' Mark said quietly.

'I don't want to live in England.' Her voice was low.

'Even though you already have Andrew's property there?'

'Yes. I'll probably rent out the cottage and the stables, but as for living there... With Andrew gone, this is the right time for me to leave and try something new.'

'You could build up something in Zimbabwe and find it wasn't what you wanted after all.'

'I don't think so, but I'm prepared to take the risk.'

'You know nothing about Africa, Tiffany. It's a beautiful continent. It's also hard and harsh and unforgiving, and you might regret giving up what you could have had.'

Caught by the seriousness in his tone, she looked back at him. Mark's eyes were bleak and impersonal, impossible to read. Tiffany felt as if he was challenging her in some way, compelling her to search deep inside herself before she made a commitment to decisions from which there would be no easy retreat.

'I really believe that this is right for me,' she said quietly.

'How can you be so sure?'

'I told you I had a dream,' she said slowly. 'I didn't tell you how I came by it. You know that I was here yesterday. I was exploring when I found an old saddle.

A name had been scratched into the leather. Andrew. It was Andrew's saddle.' Her voice was soft and wondering, and when she looked at Mark her eyes had the glow of polished emeralds. 'You may not understand this, Mark, but it came to me that Andrew wanted me to live here. I think he wanted it very much.'

If Mark was moved by her story, his expression did not show it. If anything, his eyes were more impersonal than before. 'You're about to change your life because of an old saddle?'

'It's more than that.'

'You're romanticising a coincidence.'

Tiffany was dismayed by the unyielding hardness in the square-jawed face. 'I believe it's more than coincidence,' she said urgently. 'Think of it, Mark—a saddle that hasn't been used in years, and I find it shortly after I get here. It's like a sign, an omen. It's hard to put this into words... but when I held that saddle in my arms I felt as if Andrew was telling me something.'

'Telling you what?' Mark demanded contemptuously.

'I believe he left me this house because he wanted me to make it my home.'

'Are you going to tell me he arranged to have the saddle lying where you'd find it?'

'Of course not. That part really is just amazing coincidence, and I can't begin to explain it,' Tiffany conceded. 'I can only assume that one of the tenants must have been using it, and discarded it when he moved out. But I got to thinking... Perhaps there was a reason why Andrew didn't leave this property to his relatives, a more important reason than that their relationship wasn't a close one. He gave me all he owned in England, he didn't have to give me more here. Isn't it possible that he left me this house because he wanted me to make my home in Zimbabwe?'

'If it was what he wanted, he could have told you so.'

'That wouldn't have been Andrew's way. He was a retiring, unobtrusive kind of man; he'd never come right out and tell a person what to do. You'd have to have known him to understand.'

Mark made an impatient sound in his throat. 'If you want to live here, Tiffany, that's one thing. Second-guessing Andrew's intentions is another. I still refuse to believe the man had any attachment to the place, otherwise he wouldn't have spent all his life in another country.'

'There are things you don't understand...' Tiffany began, and stopped. Even those few words were more than she had meant to say.

'You're right,' Mark said flatly, 'I don't understand how a man who had any feelings for his home and family could have cut all ties with them.'

He cut the ties because he lived all his life with the fear that his family would mock him if they learned the truth. It was a thought which Tiffany had to keep to herself.

'Andrew lived the way he felt was best for him,' she said quietly. 'His will has made it possible for me to do what is best for me.'

Mark lay back on the rug and closed his eyes, but even in repose his face had a look of concentration. Tiffany wished she had a way of peering beneath the lowered lids into his mind.

The lizard slithered over the top of the rock and vanished from sight. An exotic bird fluttered its wings in a nearby tree, then was still. A few dusty leaves dropped from the bluegums on to the ground. It was almost midday. The sky was steel-blue and cloudless, and the sun's rays were scorching.

Restlessly, Tiffany changed her position on the rug. Glancing at Mark, she saw that his expression was preoccupied; it was safe to look at him. Her eyes travelled over his calves, tanned and muscular over the narrow hips and taut thighs. This morning she had been so close to him, her body straining against his—but clothes had been a barrier. Involuntarily she wondered what it would be like to share a bed with him, to feel his nakedness against her own. To make love fully with this man whose sexuality was so pervasive, so much a part of him that his nearness made her feel raw.

Without warning, Mark opened his eyes. 'I need some answers, Tiffany.'

Caught off guard, feeling as if she had been apprehended in her moment of private scrutiny, she said, 'Ask me anything you like.'

'If I were to say yes to this idea of yours—*if*, mind you—you'd need horses.'

Tiffany forced herself to concentrate. 'Yes.'

'How many?'

She thought about that. 'Two to start with. More later, but two should be enough at the beginning.'

'The water situation leaves much to be desired.'

'There's a borehole on the property, and that should satisfy most of my needs. If it doesn't, I can make other arrangements.'

'At a cost.'

'At a cost,' Tiffany agreed, a steady look sending Mark the message that if he imagined his questions could intimidate her he was mistaken.

'Stables,' he said.

'I'll get someone to build them, but that's one cost I won't need to incur right away.'

'Why not?'

'I told you about the barn where I found Andrew's saddle. There were horses there once.'

His eyes gleamed with interest. 'How do you know?'

'There are smells I understand. I'm a horsewoman—remember?'

For the first time since they'd begun the conversation, Mark grinned. The attractive wrinkling of eyes and tilting of lips filled Tiffany with intense pleasure.

'You're also a businesswoman,' he said. 'We're talking expenses. Horses. Proper stables eventually. You'll need feed and straw, maybe water. All costing money.'

'Is there enough in the estate?'

'Probably.'

'Then there's no problem!'

Mark touched her hand, covering it with one of his. 'Don't get your hopes up yet—I haven't said yes.'

Tiffany tried to ignore the evocative feeling of long fingers on her sun-warmed skin. Keeping her voice neutral, she said, 'What else do you want to know?'

'How much do you know about running a business? Even if there's enough money in the estate now, it won't last forever. The stables would have to stand on their own.'

'I believe they would.'

He turned her hand over, and now his thumb moved tantalisingly across a sensitive palm. 'Bravado or confidence?'

Tiffany danced him a smile. 'Maybe a little of both.'

Mark's eyes lingered on her mouth a few seconds, and a muscle flicked in his jaw. The wicked thumb was creating havoc with her senses.

'You said something about a barn.'

Glad of the opportunity to create some space between them, to break a mood which she was not sure she could cope with much longer, Tiffany moved her hand away from his and rose to her feet.

'I'll show it to you.'

As they made their way around the house, Tiffany walked at a distance from Mark, not so great as to draw sardonic comment, but big enough to remove herself from a virility that was making her more aware by the second of her own sexuality. Glancing at him once, she drew an answering look of amusement. Heat rushed to her cheeks as she realised that he had noted both her distance and its purpose.

She was glad when they came to the barn. But her relief was short-lived, for Mark was not content to remain in the doorway. He wanted to explore the barn, and it was clear that he expected Tiffany to explore with him.

'Come,' he said.

She hung back. 'It's dark—and you don't have the torch with you today.'

'Dim, not dark, Tiffany. Your eyes will adjust.'

'I don't think...' she began, and stopped.

'You don't think what, Tiffany? You were here yourself yesterday—isn't this where you found the saddle?'

'It was near the doorway.'

'Do you want me to see the barn?'

'I never expected a thorough inspection; it isn't necessary. It's huge, Mark, but you can get an idea of the place without going inside.'

'That isn't my way, Tiffany. If you're going to turn the barn into stables, I need to see it properly—and I insist you see it with me.'

Still Tiffany hesitated. But she knew she was dependent on Mark Rowlands's goodwill—without it she could do nothing. And for some reason he had made up his mind to see the interior of the barn. Whether he was really interested, or whether he was simply driven by devilment, was anybody's guess. One way or another, there was nothing for it but to see the barn with him.

As Mark had predicted, her eyes adjusted to the dimness, and she looked around her with interest. Improvements were necessary, but the first horses would have a fine home here.

'I see what you mean about the horsy smell,' Mark commented wryly.

Tiffany laughed. 'Rather hits you, doesn't it? But I love it. Smells bring back memories, and all my memories of horses are happy ones.'

'Think any of the tenants ever put a broom or a bucket of water to the floor? The place would need a major clean-up before you could use it, Tiffany.'

She turned to him quickly. 'Is that a yes?'

Mark chuckled softly in the darkness. 'It means that I'm considering it.'

'Mark...'

'Don't press me on this, Tiffany. I deal with facts, not impulse or instinct. Give me time to think.'

And that, Tiffany understood, was as much as she was likely to get out of him today.

They walked further. The place really was in dire need of a good clean, she thought. Bits of old straw brushed against her ankles, and here and there her shoes encountered something slippery. 'The sooner I get——' The rest of the sentence was lost as her right foot skidded sideways. She would have fallen if Mark had not caught his arm around her waist.

'Thanks,' she said breathlessly. 'I'm not sure what happened there, but...' Her voice changed as the other arm folded around her as well. 'What are you doing?'

'What do you think?' asked Mark huskily.

'I'm fine; you can let me go now.'

'In a moment, Tiffany.'

'You've seen all you need,' she said jerkily. 'Let's get out of this place.'

'Not so fast,' he said, and drew her closer. 'I want to kiss you. I've wanted to do this all day.'

It was what she had wanted, too. The thought of their kisses had never been far from her mind.

'We were disturbed this morning, Tiffany, but there's nothing to stop us now.'

'Mark...' she whispered, but his lips stopped any words she could say.

His kisses were like none that had gone before. Hard, wild, passionate, renewing the hunger of the morning, flooding her body with desire. In seconds she was responding to him with all the ardour that was in her. One drugging kiss followed another, so that Tiffany could not have said when one kiss ended and another began. She jerked when a hand slid beneath her shirt, a small moan of delight escaping her when she felt his fingers at her breast. The other hand was moving over her, shaping itself to her neck, her waist, her hips and down over her buttocks. Achingly excited now, Tiffany let him caress her wherever he chose. There was a part of her that wished he would never stop.

After a while Mark lifted his head. 'You're so lovely,' he said raggedly. 'I can see why Andrew would have given in to you every time.'

Still dazed from his lovemaking, reeling from the unfulfilled needs of her body, Tiffany managed to look up at him. 'What are you saying?' she whispered.

'I understand Andrew. You're so beautiful, Tiffany. So seductive. You could drive a saint out of his mind with your loveliness.'

'Mark, no...' The words emerged on a wave of pain.

But he would not be stopped. As if he had not heard her protest, he said, 'It would be a strong man who could refuse you anything you wanted.'

Feeling a little ill, she tried to push herself away from him. His arms tightened around her, but she made her hands into fists and pressed them hard against his chest.

'We've just started,' he objected huskily.

'No!' she cried.

Still pushing at him, she tried to step backwards, and this time the hands that held her loosened.

'Tiffany?' He sounded puzzled. 'What's wrong? What's changed?'

Tiffany blinked back tears, thankful that it was too dark for Mark to see her pain.

'Let's get out of here,' she whispered.
'Why?' And then, on a harder note, 'You were responding to me—was that just a game?'
'No!' The word came out on a sob.
But Mark was unmoved by her distress. He was obviously very angry now. 'One minute you're a wanton, straining against me, your lips like fire. The next minute you're an outraged virgin. *Why*, Tiffany? Tell me why.'
'I didn't realise... I thought...' She swallowed hard on her tears. 'You said that Andrew...'
'What about Andrew?'
'You...you said he gave in to me... That he gave me whatever I wanted...'
'You know it's what I think.'
'How can you kiss me when you think so badly of me?'
'Does it matter? When I hold you I forget my doubts.'
'It *does* matter,' Tiffany said fiercely. 'You don't do the things we were doing unless you...' She stopped, appalled to realise how close she had come to saying the word 'love'.
'Unless?' Mark prompted.
'Unless you have trust,' she improvised dully.
'So that's what this is all about,' he said mockingly. 'Don't you know that a person's intellect and emotions are not always in sync?'
'That's a man talking,' Tiffany retorted bitterly. 'For a woman it's different.'
'We were both enjoying ourselves,' Mark said harshly.
Tiffany's face was burning, in contrast with the rest of her body which felt colder by the second.
'I didn't deny it this morning, I...I won't deny it now,' she admitted bravely. 'Maybe...maybe I did enjoy it. That doesn't stop me from wishing we had never started. You and I think differently, Mark. We react differently.'
'You're making a darn sight too much of this whole affair.' His voice was laced with contempt.

Affair... Face it, that was all it was to Mark. Sex. Chemistry. A man and a woman moving at full tilt towards the bedroom.

All of it wrong, as far as Tiffany was concerned. If she was certain of anything, it was that she could only make love with a man she loved. Just as certainly, she knew that if Mark had wanted to take her to bed she would have gone with him.

Shaken, she jerked up her head and looked at him. Her eyes had adjusted themselves sufficiently to the dimness of the barn to make out the rugged lines of Mark's face. She could see his eyes, though it was much too dark for her to see their expression, and for that she was thankful—because if she had been able to see his eyes he would have seen hers too, and he would have understood her confusion. Might even have understood the cause of it.

Dear lord, Tiffany thought, have I really fallen in love with Mark Rowlands?

She was trembling as she wheeled from him and ran from the barn. He joined her seconds later, questioning eyes searching her face. His lips parted, as if he were about to speak, but to Tiffany's relief he must have thought better of whatever it was he had intended to say, and he remained silent.

For a long moment Tiffany stared in horror at the man she had fallen in love with, a man who had never bothered to conceal his contempt. He was also still looking at her, his expression so odd, almost as if he was seeing her properly for the first time.

'What now?' he asked at last.

'Take me back to the city.' Her lips were dry and her throat hurt.

He put up no argument. Returning to the site of their picnic, they packed the basket in silence.

Five minutes later they were in the car and driving down the rutted sand road. Tiffany sat rigidly in her seat, as close to the door as she could manage. Now and then she sensed Mark glancing at her, but she kept her own eyes firmly and unseeingly on the view beyond the window.

She was not surprised when the sky turned ominously dark, and what seemed like a hurricane-force wind tore through the *veld*. The fierceness of the wind was a fitting complement to her own mood.

'Frightened?' Mark asked.

Her eyes were on the flying dust. 'Should I be?'

'It's quite a storm.'

Tiffany turned to him for the first time since they'd left the house. 'As a woman determined to make my life alone in the bush, do you really think I'd let a bit of a wind scare me?' she responded with spirit.

He laughed at that. One hand left the wheel and reached towards hers, where it lay between them on the seat. Tiffany tensed, but did not move away. At the last moment, Mark must have changed his mind. Tiffany saw his lips tighten as he returned his hand to the wheel.

By the time they reached the outskirts of the city the worst of the wind had passed, and the traffic was proceeding normally. Only Tiffany's mood was unchanged.

They were outside the hotel when Mark spoke again. 'Prepare something for me to look at.'

Her hand was on the door, ready to open it. Her head jerked around. 'Tell me what you want.'

'A presentation. Ideas. Figures. Projected profits and expenses. As detailed a presentation as you can make it.'

'When do you want to see it?'

'Whenever you're ready.'

He grinned at her then, eyes sparkling with devilment in the hard-planed face. If Mark Rowlands had any idea what his kisses had done for Tiffany's peace of mind—and how could he not?—he was clearly unrepentant.

CHAPTER FIVE

NEXT morning, Tiffany waited just long enough to buy herself a tape-measure, clipboard, notebook, pen and a large torch before taking the road that led out of the city.

Today she had little interest in the scenery. Only on the periphery of her mind did she notice the damage yesterday's wind-storm had wreaked on the countryside: branches littering the *veld*, the occasional tree with its trunk split raw, a light-standard bent double. Only the rock formations, those strange apparitions of nature, seemed untouched.

Tiffany's mouth was set in a grim line as she drove through the gates of the property towards Andrew's house. Her house now. The house where she would start a new career and a new life for herself. If, of course, the imperious Mark Rowlands gave his approval. It was up to her to convince him to give it. Just as it was up to her to forget him after that, for if she did not she was in for heartbreak. Already more than half in love with Mark, she had a sinking feeling that the second objective might be very much more difficult to achieve than the first.

Parking the car at the side of the house, she got out and stood for a minute or two in the shade of the bluegums. Already the sun's rays were beating down hard. The slight breeze that stirred the dry grass and ruffled the leaves of the trees was the only respite from the heat. Here, as everywhere else, broken branches and twigs littered the ground.

As Tiffany walked to the barn she was aware of the stillness and vastness of the countryside. The horizon seemed so distant, the cloudless sky so huge. It was all very different from the countryside she had known most of her life. England was beautiful, but this harsh, dry land was beautiful too. Beautiful in a primeval way that enthralled the eye and excited the senses. Andrew must have known that she would love it.

In the doorway of the barn she stopped, the memory of yesterday's kisses making her feel weak for a moment.

'No,' she said aloud in the stillness, 'I will *not* think about Mark.' And she flicked on her torch and walked inside.

The next few hours were spent measuring, calculating, pondering how the barn could best be partitioned, wondering how many horses could comfortably be stabled there.

It was a little before midday when she returned to Bulawayo. Finding a restaurant in one of the side streets, she ordered coffee and a toasted cheese sandwich, and then she took out her notebook and began to write.

Her order arrived, and she sipped her coffee without looking up from her work. Had she done so, she might have observed the appreciative glances thrown her way by several of the restaurant's male patrons. Then again, they might not have meant much to her. Tiffany had never thought of herself as pretty: it would not have occurred to her to wonder if men had noticed her. Her thoughts were concentrated solely on her work.

After lunch she returned to the hotel and spent the afternoon in her room, making telephone calls. Calls to carpenters and electricians, to companies that sold feed and hay, to ranches that might have horses for sale. In her notebook, the pages filled up, pages covered with figures and diagrams.

One minute after eight o'clock the next morning, Tiffany phoned Mark.

'Rose nymph—were you watching the time? I've just walked into the office.'

His voice came to her through the line, low and attractive, and so vital that she felt as if he were in the room with her.

'I want to see you, Mark,' she said.

'You're inviting me to lunch?'

Tiffany closed her eyes at the teasing note in his voice. How she wished there was some consistency to the man. If he was always arrogant, that she could endure—somehow. At least she'd know where she stood with him. But Mark was mercurial: tough lawyer and cynic one minute, seductive flirt the next. With Mark Rowlands she never knew what to expect.

'My presentation is ready,' she told him, ignoring his question.

'Fast work,' he answered her drily. 'You must want those stables very badly.'

'I do. I'm hoping you'll be impressed.'

'Won't know until I see what you have for me. Tell you what, Tiffany, you can show it to me over lunch. My treat, and I know just the place—secluded alcoves, great guitar player, and delicious food to boot.'

'No...' she said unsteadily.

'No?' He pretended astonishment. 'You're not tempted?'

Oh, yes, she was tempted. Too much so, that was the problem. Tiffany could picture the place. Soft music, hushed voices. Intimacy. Mark in his most infuriatingly seductive mood, making her fall more deeply in love with him by the second. And then, when he had melted her, softened her with his romantic wizardry, his mood would change. She would show him her presentation, and he would crush her with his arrogance and his baseless accusations.

No... If she was going to do battle with him—and battle was likely wherever they met—it was important to talk in an atmosphere where she could maintain a clear head.

'Let's meet across a desk,' she said.

'You really are scared of me.' He sounded amused.

Her hand tightened on the receiver. 'I've told you before that I'm not. This is business, Mark, and our discussion should take place in your office.'

'Did Andrew know this prissy side of you?' A mocking laugh. 'Don't bother answering; the question was rhetorical. Be here around five.'

She glanced at her watch as she put down the phone. Eight hours to wait... And she looked around the room restlessly, and wished that the thought of seeing Mark again were not so important to her.

Eight hours to fill. Nothing but futile daydreams to fill them with. She sat up at the sound of a vacuum cleaner outside her door. In the past, she had always found physical work an effective antidote to worry or boredom; it would be that again now.

On her bed lay the jade dress and black patent shoes she'd planned to wear for her meeting with Mark. It took her only a minute or two to pack them into her small overnight case, along with a brush and comb and some make-up. That done, she pulled on jeans, a T-shirt and sandals, and carried the case out of the hotel.

Stopping only to buy a broom, a mop and a few bottles of detergent, Tiffany navigated the car out of the city. The road was so familiar by now that she was able to lop ten minutes off her drive to the house.

Once there, she assessed it critically. The place was a mess, she decided, but she knew what to do about it.

She set to cleaning with a vigour that was fuelled as much by the need to make the house habitable as by the determination not to let herself think about Mark. When she straightened her aching back and looked around a few hours later, she knew that she had satisfied at least one of her objectives. There was a lot more to be done in the house, but at least the main bedroom, the kitchen and a bathroom were fit to be used.

When she had changed into the jade dress she glanced at herself in the bathroom mirror. Earlier that day the glass had been thick with grime, but now her reflection looked back at her. Loosening her hair from the pony-tail she'd worn while working, she brushed it until it fell in soft waves around her head. Just a few days in Africa, and already her face had a soft apricot colour. Freckles dusted her cheeks and nose, and her green eyes glowed—she barely needed the extra colour of make-up.

This time, when she emerged from the lift on the ninth floor and walked into the wide-windowed waiting area, the girl at the desk was expecting her.

'Mr Rowlands's last client has just left, Miss Marlow, so you can go right in.'

'Thank you,' Tiffany returned with a smile.

But as she walked down the passage towards Mark's office, nervousness was causing her heart to beat a little too fast. It was so important that he say yes to her proposal.

He rose from his chair and came to meet her, and for a moment Tiffany could only look at him wordlessly, her resolve not to be affected by him vanishing, blown away like petals in a wind. Autocratic Mark might be; at the same time no other man had ever made her feel so feminine, so desirable, quite so vibrantly alive.

'Hello, rose nymph.'

The way he said the nickname he had made so peculiarly his own sounded like an endearment, a kiss, a caress. It filled her with intense pleasure.

'Hello, Mark,' she said softly.

His eyes moved over her in a look that was unmistakably male. 'You look very lovely.'

'Thank you.'

'You can still change your mind, you know. We could go to that restaurant I mentioned earlier.'

'I'd rather not,' she said unsteadily.

He looked down at her, his eyes hooded suddenly and unreadable. Then his hand touched her cheek in a disturbingly sensual gesture.

'I'm your trustee; you're not going to be able to avoid me indefinitely.'

Tiffany was conscious of a vulnerability that had no place in this office. A faint flush warmed her cheeks, but she was able to say calmly, 'Once my plans get off the ground, it won't be necessary for us to meet. At least not often. I may have to ask you for money, but we can probably settle most things over the phone.'

A hint of mockery touched his eyes. 'All right, Tiffany, sit down, and we'll talk.'

Tension was making her tremble a little as she sat down. She was all too aware of how much depended on what was said here today. But by the time Mark had walked around his desk and sat down too, she had managed to gain some semblance of control.

'Tell me about the stables,' he invited.

She passed the sand-coloured folder to him. 'It's all there.'

She watched as he opened the folder and began to leaf through the sheaf of papers. Her eyes went from his hands—hands which could do such unnerving things to her senses—to his face. So absorbed was Mark in the material she had given him that it was safe to watch him without being noticed. There was intelligence in that face, a look of competence which would inspire any potential client with trust. Strength too. Give Mark Rowlands a complex case, one that seemed destined for failure, and he would fight it with courage and daring. He was a man who would rise to any challenge, Tiffany guessed. A finger of dark hair fell over his forehead, and she ached with the need to push it gently back where it belonged.

Suddenly he lifted his head. There was a speculative expression in his eyes, and Tiffany knew that her scrutiny had not gone unnoticed after all. For a long moment his eyes held hers. Then he gestured towards the folder.

'Interesting.'

Tiffany leaned forward eagerly. 'Do you really mean that?'

'I never say anything I don't mean.'

'You've said more than once that you consider me a schemer.'

'I have, haven't I?'

'You've made no secret of the fact that you think I talked Andrew into making me his beneficiary.'

'Correct.'

Disappointment created a sour taste in her mouth. She wished that Mark's opinion did not matter so much to her.

'Maybe I shouldn't have come here after all,' she said slowly.

'I've said other things too,' he reminded her softly. 'I've told you that you're beautiful. That you're desirable. I've made no secret of the fact that you excite me enormously.'

'In a physical sense only.' The words were out before she could stop them; she would have liked to take them back the moment they escaped her lips.

He shot her a mocking grin. 'What do you expect from a man, Tiffany? An offer of marriage just because he makes it plain he'd like to go to bed with you?'

Her fingers dug deep into the soft palms of her hands. 'Has anyone ever told you that you're arrogant?'

'You have, several times. Why the question, anyway? Because I tell the truth?'

'The truth as *you* see it,' she said furiously.

'Maybe so. I believe you're a woman who wants things from a man. You wanted things—and got them—from Andrew. What do you want from me, Tiffany?'

She knew very well what she wanted from him. Love. Trust. Commitment. A lifetime of sharing, nights spent in the same bed. She stared at him, her eyes dazed with shock, horrified by the moment of insight. She'd known yesterday that she loved him. Yet, sensing danger perhaps, she had now allowed herself the freedom of such detailed thoughts—until this moment. And she knew that Mark must have no inkling of what was on her mind, for if he did he would become even more insolent than he was already.

'I only want one thing from you—your consent to go ahead with the stables,' she said blindly, wondering how it was possible to hate a man at the same time as she loved him. She swallowed hard. 'You haven't said what you think of the proposal.'

'I did tell you. It's interesting. All these facts and figures and diagrams surpass anything I expected.'

Hope brightened her eyes. 'Does that mean I have your consent?'

'I'll need to check these figures first.'

'You'll find them correct.'

He grinned at her. 'Perhaps. You've given me some intriguing material, and now I need time to evaluate it. I'm a lawyer, Tiffany. I know you'd like me to give you an answer on the spot, but that's not my way. I can't rush things without being certain of the facts. You understand that, don't you?'

'Yes.' Her voice was low with disappointment.

'I'll phone you when I have something to tell you.'

'That won't be possible. I'll have to phone you.'

'Going somewhere?' He was studying her speculatively.

'Home.'

'*Home*?' He looked startled. 'You're going back to England?'

'Home being my new house,' Tiffany told him with immense relish.

An expression came and went in his eyes, as if, just for a moment, Mark Rowlands had been faced with a situation he did not like at all, as if he was relieved to find he had been wrong.

'You're moving into Andrew's house?' he asked then.

'Yes.'

'Without waiting for my reaction to your proposal?'

'It's my house; I don't need your consent to live in it,' she said spiritedly. 'You may as well know, Mark, that I intend to go ahead with the stables. With your consent or without it. Your consent would make things a lot easier for me, of course, but if you decide to withhold the money I'll approach a bank for a loan.'

'When did you make this decision?'

'A few seconds ago.'

Thoughtful eyes scanned her face. 'And when are you moving?'

'Tomorrow morning.'

'The house is a mess, Tiffany.'

'Not as much of a mess as it was when you saw it. I spent the day cleaning. I've just come from there.'

His eyes dropped from her face to her body. 'Cleaning—in that dress?' he asked disbelievingly.

There was so much masculine appreciation in his gaze that Tiffany laughed in delight. 'In jeans and a T-shirt, actually. I packed the dress in the car when I left the hotel.'

As he lifted his head, his expression changed. For the first time Tiffany thought she saw respect in his eyes.

'Where will you sleep?' he asked after a moment. 'On one of the mattresses used by the tenants? Somehow I don't believe you'd enjoy that.'

She threw him a sparkling look. 'I've bought myself a sleeping-bag.'

'Well!' Suddenly he smiled, a smile that lifted his lips and warmed his eyes, a smile that made its way directly to Tiffany's heart. 'You're a feisty girl,' he said. 'Head-strong, argumentative, single-minded and stubborn.'

'More qualities of mine that you detest?'

'On the contrary—I admire them.'

Remembering that he always meant the things he said, Tiffany experienced a surge of pure happiness. Then she remembered those other things he had said—and meant—and she got up.

'Goodbye, Mark. I'll phone you next week. I hope you'll have an answer for me by then.'

For a few seconds Tiffany did not know where she was or what had woken her. Groping fingers encountered a slippery fabric that was unlike the eiderdown in Andrew's cottage, unlike the blankets at the hotel. She remained puzzled until the hardness beneath her back reminded her that all there was between her body and the floor was the lining of her sleeping-bag, and that the walls she saw were the walls of her new home.

With a sigh of satisfaction, she stretched luxuriously and opened her eyes. Through the uncurtained window she could see the sky, a little grey still in the early dawn. Birds sang in the branches of the bluegums beside the house, calling morning greetings to each other and making plans for the day, Tiffany thought with an amused smile.

Bird-watching was one of her favourite pastimes. Andrew had always put out feed, and summer and winter there had been a pageant of birds in his garden. After just a few days in Zimbabwe, Tiffany had noticed that there were species here which she had not known in England. One of her first purchases would be a book about the birds of Africa, she decided. She would put a feeder near the house and spend time getting to know the birds that flew in the *veld*, and then——

Her smile vanished as a harsh noise intruded on her thoughts. Tnis was what must have woken her.

The noise stopped, only to begin once more seconds later. A scraping kind of noise, as if something heavy were being dragged along the ground. Along the floor... *Inside the house*! An icy shiver ran down Tiffany's spine as she remembered that her nearest neighbours were so far away that however loudly she screamed they would not hear her.

It took less than a quarter of a minute for her to thrust aside the folds of the sleeping-bag, leap to her feet and run to the door. Only to find that if ever there had been a key in the lock, it was no longer there now.

The scraping noise was louder now. Approaching Tiffany's room. Frenziedly, she looked around her. She was dragging a dresser towards the door when she saw the knob turn.

She had always possessed the ability to think quickly. She thought quickly now. On top of the dresser was a ceramic vase which she had bought in Bulawayo just yesterday, and which she had filled with dry pods and wild grasses from the garden. Standing back against the wall, she held the vase at shoulder level, ready to aim it at the intruder's head.

The door opened halfway, pushed against the dresser, stopped, pushed further. Tiffany saw a tanned hand go to the dresser for a final shove. A second later a man appeared in the doorway.

'*Mark*!' The shock of relief made Tiffany weak. Her body was damp with perspiration.

'Who were you expecting this time, rose nymph? A waiter with a breakfast tray all the way from Bulawayo?'

Mark's eyes sparkled with amusement as he took in the vase and the raised hand. 'What on earth are you doing with that thing? I thought I was safe after I stopped you from decapitating me with a paperweight—were you really going to hurl that vase at my head?'

'If necessary,' she said breathlessly. 'Good lord, Mark, I thought you were a burglar or a rapist. You're lucky I *didn't* throw the vase at you.'

'You're very pale,' he said in a new voice.

'No wonder—you frightened me.'

'I'm sorry,' he said softly, as he closed the distance between them and drew her to him.

She was trembling so violently now that she had neither the strength nor the will to resist him. There was, in fact, something intensely comforting in the feel of the strong arms holding her, in the warmth of the hard body against hers, in the male smell that filled her nostrils.

The trembling did not last long. Tiffany's body quietened, but the need to stay in Mark's arms remained. When he bent his head to kiss her she did not draw away from him. For a minute, at least, she was kissing him back. And then she remembered that this man meant only trouble. It took a supreme effort of will on her part, but she managed to push herself away from him.

'How did you get in?' she demanded.

'I had a spare key.'

'Did you think that gave you the right to walk in? This is my house now, Mark, and I value my privacy. Couldn't you have knocked?'

'Actually, I knocked a few times, but there was no answer.'

She had woken after he was already in the house, Tiffany realised, not surprisingly perhaps, because she had always been a sound sleeper. She would have to put bolts on the doors, and soon. The next intruder could be more dangerous than Mark Rowlands.

'You could have let me know you were coming,' she accused.

'You don't have a phone,' he reminded her drily.

'Not yet... But even then, you...'

She began to tremble once more as she saw his gaze leave her face and descend to her body, so intensely that it was as if he were making love to her with his eyes. For the first time she remembered that she had been so tired by the time she'd finished in the house the previous night that she had gone to sleep in bikini bra and panties rather than take the time to unpack her suitcase.

A hand went up in a kind of self-defence. 'Don't look at me like that,' she pleaded.

'Do you have any idea how sexy you are?' he asked huskily.

'Don't start something . . . please . . .' Both hands were at her breasts now, as if somehow she could hide them.

'We already did. Or did you think nothing of those kisses?'

They had made her yearn for a more complete love-making. For the fulfilment that only Mark would be able to give her. At the same time she understood that it would be folly to encourage him.

'What I meant is...we mustn't lose control.' Her voice shook.

'We lost control some time ago. We want each other, Tiffany. You're lying to yourself if you try to tell yourself otherwise.'

His hands covered hers, his warmth communicating itself through skin and nerve and sinew to her breasts.

'You shouldn't be ashamed of how you look,' he said softly. 'You should celebrate your desirability.'

'*Celebrate*?' She looked at him incredulously. She had never known a man who spoke like Mark Rowlands.

'Celebrate, rose nymph. But only with me.' His eyes gleamed possessively.

'What are you saying?' she whispered.

'That you're the most desirable woman I've ever met. You know very well that I'm attracted to you.'

It was hard to swallow on a dry throat. 'If I'd known you were coming, I'd have been fully dressed.'

'It wouldn't have made any difference. You'd be sexy in sackcloth, Tiffany. I see you and I want to make love to you.'

The hunger within her was becoming an intense physical ache. 'But you haven't changed your mind about me...'

'I've thought you desirable from the moment we met.'

'I'm talking about Andrew.' She moistened her lips with her tongue. 'The inheritance...'

'That,' Mark said dismissively. 'Why bring it up now?'

Anger flooded her being, white-hot, searing. Tiffany folded her arms tightly around herself. 'Get out!' she ordered, backing away from him.

'You and I are going to make love.'

'We'll do nothing of the kind.'

'I've even brought the wherewithal.'

'*What*?' she exclaimed, outraged.

Mark laughed. 'What I meant was that I've brought you a bed. It's in the passage.'

So that accounted for the scraping sounds that had woken her—Mark must have been dragging a bed through the house.

'This is my home now, and I don't want you in it,' she said hardily. 'Please go.'

'Where do you want it? Under the window or against the wall?'

Briefly her eyes went to the ceramic vase, but she rejected that option. 'I don't think you heard me,' she said tensely.

'It's a heavy bed, Tiffany. I want it in the right position the first time.'

'I don't want it at all. I'm perfectly comfortable in my sleeping-bag.'

His gaze went to the crumpled folds on the floor. When he looked at her again, there was a gleam in his eyes. 'You wouldn't mind sharing your sleeping quarters with a spider or a scorpion?'

Tiffany suppressed a shudder. 'You're trying to frighten me. There might be scorpions in the bush, but there are none in the house.'

'You'd be a lot better off on a bed than on the ground, Tiffany.'

'I have every intention of buying my own furniture,' she said unsteadily.

'It's Saturday today. Even if you drove into the city right now, you'd still have to wait until next week for delivery.'

'I don't mind waiting.'

'I do.'

She looked at him disbelievingly. 'You think so little of me, Mark; why would you care if something happened to me?'

He looked at her a long moment, and she waited breathlessly for his reply. But when he spoke his voice was without expression. 'You're new here; it will take a while before you understand the ways of the bush. I'm your trustee—is it so strange that I should feel some responsibility for you?'

Fool that she'd been to ask the question! Hoping to hear words that Mark would never say. What was wrong with her anyway, allowing herself to fall in love with a man who would never bring her anything but heartache?

She treated him to her coldest look. 'You're only responsible for my money, and as far as I'm concerned someone else could take care of that as well as you. I know you've come out a long way to bring me this bed, Mark, but I don't want it or need it. If some rotten spider or scorpion is stupid enough to come my way, I'll give it short shrift. So—I appreciate the effort, but you've wasted your time.' She lifted her chin at him. 'Now will you go?'

'No.'

'*What does it take to get through to you*?'

'Would you be interested if I told you the bed wasn't the only reason I came here today?' Laziness in his tone, sheer wickedness in his expression.

She looked at him warily. 'There's another reason?'

'Remember a certain presentation?'

Tiffany drew a swift breath. 'You've looked at it already?'

'Yes.'

'But I only brought it to you yesterday. I didn't think...' The blood was drumming in her veins.

'I have an answer for you,' Mark said, and cupped her chin in his hand.

She forced herself to stand very still. Through dry lips, she said, 'Don't keep me in suspense.'

The eyes that rested on her face were deep and steady, their gaze penetrating. Not for the first time, Tiffany had the disturbing feeling that Mark could see through skin and bone to the very core of her being.

'You can have your stables,' he said at last.

Wordlessly she stared at him, her lips trembling, her eyes sparkling with a sheen that made the watching man think of jewels.

A thumb moved downwards over her throat. 'It means so much to you?' There was a note in Mark's tone which Tiffany had not heard before.

'It means everything,' she said simply.

Mark seemed to make a sound in his throat. Then his hand left her face, dropping abruptly to his side.

When he spoke again, his tone was unusually detached. 'On Monday I'll get the bank to arrange a line of credit for you. You won't have to come to me every time you need money.'

The words should have thrilled her. Independent woman that Tiffany was, the idea of seeking her trustee's approval before every purchase or decision was galling. Yet the thought that her contact with Mark Rowlands was about to end was even more disquieting.

'Wonderful,' she said brightly. 'Then I can get started with my plans on Monday.'

His lips lifted slightly at the corners. 'Better than that—you can start today.'

'I don't understand...'

'On my way out I passed some signs. There's an agricultural fair not far from here. You could look at some horses, get an idea of what's available.'

'I'd like that very much. Will you tell me how to get there?'

'I'll take you there myself—but get some clothes on first.' The last words were spoken in a dry tone.

Incredibly, Tiffany had forgotten her near-naked state. She looked down at herself, seeing her body as Mark must see it: the soft swell of her breasts above the lacy bra, the small waist, the curved line of her hips in the high-cut bikini panties, the smoothness of slender thighs. Face flushed, she looked back at him.

'Wait for me outside,' she ordered unsteadily.

'As long as you understand that I'll be back in this room.'

'Mark...'

'You haven't seen the bed yet.'

'I don't want to.'

'A double bed, Tiffany.'

'Single is sufficient for my needs.' She tried, and knew she failed, to sound convincingly flippant.

'But not for mine.' An insolent gaze raked her body. 'I'll bring the bed into the room now, before you get dressed. Unless you have other ideas, I'll put it under the window.' He grinned at her, one of his most wicked grins. 'We'll be able to look at the stars when we make love. Because you can be sure of one thing, rose nymph—one day we will lie in that bed together.'

CHAPTER SIX

THEY were among the earlier arrivals at the fair. Mark was driving a station wagon today, and he found parking easily in the visitors' parking field. The exhibitors' parking, on the other side of the fence, was already filled with jeeps and trucks and trailers for carrying animals.

In the fairgrounds men and women in jeans and broad-brimmed hats moved around purposefully, milking cows, grooming horses, leading pigs and sheep to viewing enclosures, replacing old hay, replenishing drinking water. Children were everywhere, some helping with chores, others having a marvellous time running around with their friends.

Tiffany walked beside Mark, an unconscious lift in her step. She saw the looks that came his way from women who were obviously taken with his ruggedly handsome appearance. She was less aware of the men glancing her own way, attracted by the soft curves of her slender body and the vitality in her small heart-shaped face. She only knew that, for all that she might try to deny the fact to herself, she was intensely happy in Mark's company.

Turning from a pen of squealing piglets, she looked at him with sparkling eyes. 'There's something about country fairs, isn't there? The animals, all spruced up for the occasion. The farmers and the excited children. All that straw and hay underfoot.'

Mark grinned at her. 'The noise and the dust and the smells.'

'Yes!' She was warmed as much by his smile as by the lovely sense of something shared.

His hand went out, and she stood very still as he traced a light path from her eyes to her lips. For a few seconds she was oblivious to the noise and activity all around them; there was only the man and the hunger his touch aroused in her.

At that moment an animal dashed past them, a wayward calf, darting erratically this way and that. Behind it, in hot pursuit, came a little boy. Tears ran down his cheeks as he shouted, 'Whoa! Whoa!' but it was evident that the calf was too fast for him.

Mark reacted with a speed Tiffany had not guessed he possessed. In seconds he had caught up with the playful animal, and was looping the rope that was around its neck over his hand. Half a minute later, with a few comforting words, he was putting the rope in the grateful child's hand.

'Well!' Tiffany said, when the little boy was gone.

'Well, what?'

'I'm impressed.'

Mark looked amused. 'Because I can run faster than a child?'

'Not exactly...' Tiffany stopped, a little hesitant about putting her thoughts into words.

'You see me only as a desk-bound lawyer. In no shape to corner a runaway animal.'

She shot him a mischievous grin. 'Something like that.'

He stood very close to her, laughing down at her. In fact, even before she'd seen him catch the calf, Tiffany had recognised that today Mark was not the sophisticated lawyer she had argued with in a glass and chrome city building. Dressed in a red and white checked shirt and jeans that moulded themselves to his hips and thighs, he could easily have been taken for a cowboy. The top buttons of his shirt were open, so that Tiffany could see the strong thrust of a tanned throat and the dark hair that curled on his chest.

'Don't be too impressed, Tiffany, it was only a calf.' He was still laughing. 'Besides, don't you remember me telling you that I grew up on a farm? I was helping with the animals long before I ever saw the inside of a courtroom.'

And, with that, the episode was over. In Mark's mind, at least. As far as Tiffany was concerned, she had a feeling she would remember it for some time. Not too long though, she admonished herself wryly, knowing how stupid it was to dwell on a man whose only concern with her—apart from an undeniable physical chemistry—was as trustee of the money she had inherited.

But Mark was a difficult man to ignore. He had surprised Tiffany more than once today. At the enclosure where the horses were being shown, he was to surprise her again. Tiffany had brought along paper and a pen, and she made notes not only of her own observations but also of Mark's comments. Perceptive comments from a man who clearly knew horses well, who could tell the difference between quality and mediocrity, who seemed to understand Tiffany's requirements without her having to explain them to him.

After a while, having jotted down as much as she needed, Tiffany put her notebook back in her bag. Side by side, arms leaning on the wooden fence of the enclosure, Tiffany and Mark watched the horses being shown.

And then Mark moved, and suddenly his arm lay against Tiffany's. A hunger that was fast becoming familiar started inside her, and she had to stop herself from caressing the little hairs that stirred against her skin. She thought of moving away from him, but she knew that her turmoil would amuse him, and so she made herself stay where she was.

'See anything that interests you?' he asked.

'Quite a lot; there are some lovely animals here.'

'And you've made notes of names and prices.'

'Yes—though I won't make any purchases just yet.'

'Wise decision.'

'No sense in making a move until I'm ready.'

'Will you know when you're ready, Tiffany?' he asked, so oddly that her head jerked up. 'Will you?' That same strange tone.

Tiffany suspected that Mark was no longer talking about horses.

Abruptly, she moved her arm away from his. 'I usually know what I want,' she said unsteadily.

Earlier his laughter had been one of amusement; now it was huskily seductive. 'I'm glad to hear it,' came his soft response.

Tiffany was glad when they left the enclosure. As they walked further she made a point of widening the space between Mark and herself. Trapped in a situation beyond her control—hell to be in love with a man who would derive enormous satisfaction out of playing with her emotions—it seemed important to put some distance between them.

The fairground was more crowded now, bustling with activity and sound, and though Tiffany's main interest was horses she enjoyed seeing other livestock as well. Once, when they stopped to watch a sheep-shearing competition, onlookers loudly urging perspiring shearers to complete their tests in record time, she looked at Mark and saw that he was enjoying the competition as much as she was.

Tiffany stopped when they came to a stall stocked with colourful straw hats. 'Just what I need in this pitiless climate!' she exclaimed. It took her a few minutes to make a choice, but she settled eventually on a floppy creation with bright strands of red and yellow woven into its brim. She paid for the hat and perched it on her head there and then, laughing as she turned back to Mark.

He was still standing where she had left him, but he was no longer alone. He was in conversation with a tall woman in a scarlet trouser-suit.

Tiffany paused uncertainly, her laughter vanishing as she wondered whether she should join them, or wait until they had finished talking. But Mark had seen her.

'Tiffany,' he called, and the woman turned. Tiffany recognised her immediately.

'Miss Donaldson,' she said, forcing a smile to conceal the sinking feeling in her stomach. 'We met the other day...'

'I remember,' Clarissa said coldly.

As before, she looked stunning. Her rich blonde hair was beautifully styled, her make-up immaculate. In Mark's office she had not looked out of place; in these rustic surroundings she reminded Tiffany of some rare and beautiful bird preening itself in a gathering of humble sparrows. A little ruefully, Tiffany cast a quick glance down at her own jeans and T-shirt.

Clarissa looked at Mark. 'You forgot to mention that you were here with Uncle Andrew's little assistant. I must say, darling, I'm rather surprised—your taste in women is usually more sophisticated. Did you feel you had to treat Miss Marlow to the kind of entertainment to which she is accustomed? Noble of you, darling, but exceeding your scope of duties just a little, wouldn't you say?'

Tiffany clenched her hands tightly. Angry words came to her lips, but one look at Clarissa's provocative expression made her understand that the other woman wanted her to discredit herself by lashing out and saying things she might later regret.

With an effort of will she forced the words back. Unclenching her hands, she managed another smile instead. 'Actually,' she said disarmingly, 'Mark offered to help me set up my business.'

'A business in England, I take it,' Clarissa said frostily.

'In Zimbabwe, as a matter of fact.'

Clarissa's poise gave way to astonishment. 'In Zimbabwe—but why? Won't it be a nuisance running it long-distance?'

'I'll be running it from here.'

A slight flush appeared in the perfect face. 'Do you mean to say you'll be living here?'

'Exactly.' Tiffany spoke the word with zest.

Clarissa's lips tightened. 'What kind of business?' she demanded.

'I'm surprised Mark didn't tell you about it, but I suppose there wasn't time. I'm starting some stables, Miss Donaldson.'

'*Stables*? Where?'

'My place.'

'By that, I suppose you mean my Uncle Andrew's property.'

'As I said—my place,' Tiffany responded evenly.

Mark spoke for the first time. 'You and Clarissa share a common interest, Tiffany. Clarissa loves horses too; she's involved with show-jumping.'

Glancing at him, Tiffany saw amusement in his eyes—but there was something else as well. Admiration for the way she was standing up to the other woman? she wondered.

That look gave Tiffany the courage to say, 'I'll be taking in horses, Miss Donaldson. You might even be interested in stabling an animal with me some day.'

'Hardly.' This was Clarissa at her haughtiest once more. 'I demand the highest standards for my horses. I wouldn't dream of stabling an animal with anyone unless I was certain it would receive the best care.'

Tiffany merely smiled.

And then Clarissa was turning away from her and back to Mark. 'Have to go now, darling, but we'll catch up on things at the ball on Monday night, won't we?'

Mark nodded.

'Formal wear, of course, darling. Did I tell you I'd bought a new gown for the occasion? Very alluring—I remember you telling me once that you adored me in red. We'll have a nightcap at my place afterwards. And then, who knows...?' She threw him an invitingly flirtatious look. 'Till Monday, darling.'

Clarissa looked back at Tiffany, the kind of look that said she had belatedly remembered Tiffany's existence. 'Goodbye, Miss Marlow.' Her eyes were chips of ice.

Tiffany saw how Mark watched Clarissa walking away, blonde hair a glossy curtain about her head, hips swaying seductively. On his face was an expression Tiffany had not seen before, one she did not understand. Nor did she want to understand it, she told herself numbly. If only she had not fallen in love with him—Mark Rowlands with his kisses and caresses, and another woman in his life.

Only when Clarissa was lost in the crowds did Mark turn back to Tiffany. His face wore an oddly brooding expression now, and for a moment he regarded Tiffany almost as if she were a stranger.

And then a new expression appeared, and suddenly he was looking at her with the eyes of a lover, the intensity of his gaze like a sensuous caress on her lips and cheeks and throat. The intimacy of that look forced the colour from Tiffany's cheeks.

'Rose nymph,' he said, his voice low and husky with blatant invitation.

'No...' She took a step away from him.

'No?' he repeated, very softly. 'What is it you're saying no to?'

Tiffany's lips were dry. 'I won't go to bed with you.'

His eyes gleamed. 'Was that my question?'

She felt very stupid suddenly. Angry too. Anger gave her the strength to break the spell he was weaving around her.

'Hasn't that been the question all along?' she demanded. 'That's why you brought me the bed. You couldn't care less whether my sleeping-bag is safe or not.'

'I do care, Tiffany. It's also true I said we'd share the bed some day. I still say so.'

'Sex!' She flung the word at him furiously.

'Yes.'

'It's what you're after with every woman you meet.'

His lips tightened. 'Is that what you think?'

'What else can I think? Clarissa. Me. How many other women, Mark?'

'You're making assumptions, Tiffany.'

'Maybe I am.'

'And I think you're forgetting that my life didn't begin the day you arrived in Zimbabwe.'

'Obviously not,' she said, as coolly as she could, and wondered if he had any idea how much he was hurting her.

'There are women who——'

'I'm not interested in your women,' she interrupted him harshly. 'I don't care who they are or what you do with them. I just want you to know that this particular woman has no interest in being added to your list of conquests.'

Once more their eyes met and held. Tiffany saw a little muscle move in Mark's throat. And then, unexpectedly, his expression changed yet again. His lips tilted and his eyes held an unholy gleam.

'I hear you,' he said.

They stopped at the cafeteria before leaving the fairground. Tiffany would have been just as happy to go straight back to the house, but Mark insisted they have something to eat first.

The main portion of the cafeteria was in a large tent, but there was another smaller area outside. Mark spotted a recently vacated table in the shade, and Tiffany, still not accustomed to the intense noontime heat, sat down gratefully.

Hardly had their food been placed before them—a delicious mixture of mangoes, peaches and golden pawpaw topped with a scoop of vanilla ice-cream—when a shadow fell across the table.

'If it isn't Mark Rowlands,' a male voice said.

Looking up at an attractive man with fair hair and laughing blue eyes, Tiffany heard Mark say, 'Morning, Brent.' The words sounded clipped.

'You are going to introduce me, aren't you?'

'Brent Sawyer—Tiffany Marlow.'

'So this is the heiress,' Brent said.

'Heiress?' Tiffany repeated, a little taken aback, and saw Mark's eyes harden.

'A very beautiful heiress.' Brent's voice was husky with laughter. 'Now I understand why the lady Clarissa was in such a snit when I saw her.'

'You're embarrassing Miss Marlow,' Mark reproached the man curtly.

'Are you embarrassed, Tiffany? I think not. I've noticed that women appreciate compliments about their beauty—especially when they happen to be true.'

Blue eyes shone with mischief. Clearly, Brent Sawyer did not intend to be taken seriously. Tiffany found herself laughing back at him.

'You say you've heard about me?'

'In some detail. Word spreads quickly hereabouts, particularly when the bearer of tidings is Clarissa Donaldson. I met up with her not fifteen minutes ago, near the pig-pens I believe, and she told me everything. Heiress to all that Andrew Donaldson possessed. About to launch into the stable business. I gather Tiffany is your client, Mark, which according to the lady Clarissa is the reason you've accompanied her here today. The only reason? That was what Clarissa would have me believe, but her anger made me guess otherwise. Of course, now that I've seen the lovely Tiffany for myself, I know that I was right. Say, Mark, any time you find yourself too busy to handle Tiffany's affairs, send her my way, will you?'

'Are you a lawyer too, Mr Sawyer?' Tiffany asked.

'Brent, fair lady, Brent. I'd give you my card, but my colleague here might consider that unethical.' He looked pointedly at the empty chair which he had not been invited to use. 'I'll be on my way now. You'll find my name in the telephone directory, Tiffany—don't hesitate to phone if you should need my services.'

In a swift movement he bent, took one of Tiffany's hands, turned it over and kissed it. With a last laughing look at them both, he was gone.

'Why didn't you invite him to join us?' Tiffany asked, when Brent was out of earshot.

Mark stabbed his fork into a sliver of mango. 'I saw no reason to.'

'I gather you don't like Brent?'

'I detest the man,' Mark said shortly.

'I thought he was rather charming.'

'Charm is Brent Sawyer's stock-in-trade,' Mark answered her grimly. 'It might interest you to know that he is totally without scruples when it comes to his dealings with women.'

'Then the two of you must have things in common in addition to the practice of law. But you're not a woman, Mark, which makes me wonder—is there another reason why you dislike him so much? Have the two of you crossed swords in court?'

'Naturally, but that in itself doesn't make for bad feelings. Lawyers do battle for their clients all the time, and remain friends outside the courtroom. This is something else. Brent Sawyer happens to be a man I particularly despise. He's devious, he resorts to underhand tactics, he manipulates people and events. He stops at nothing to get what he wants.'

'Making us two of a kind?' she taunted.

Mark's sole reply was a swift hard look.

'Do you see Brent Sawyer and me as soulmates? Two peas in the same pod?'

'I didn't make the comparison, Tiffany, you did,' Mark said harshly.

'All the same, it's what you believe, isn't it?'

Glancing across the table at Mark, Tiffany saw intense anger in his face. His skin was stretched tight as a mask over his high cheekbones; his jawline had never looked quite so hard.

Tiffany's throat was dry with tension, but there was a devil that drove her to continue. 'From the beginning you've seen me as a manipulator; the thought never leaves your mind.'

Mark did not answer, and after a moment Tiffany pushed her plate away. The food was delicious, but she had lost her taste for it.

'Take me home,' she said, and got abruptly to her feet.

Tiffany got up very early on Monday morning. On Saturday and again last night she had spurned the bed which Mark had brought her, choosing to curl up in her sleeping-bag instead. Mark's talk of spiders and scorpions had been nothing more than baseless scare tactics, she had told herself grimly while giving the bag a good shaking out in the yard. Not an insect was to be seen, either in the bag or on the floor of her room, which she had inspected with a thorough eye before retiring.

Half an hour after rising, she sat at the scrubbed kitchen table and made a list of all the tasks that needed to be done that day. It was a list which, in normal circumstances, might have been daunting. As it was, Tiffany was glad of the day's chores. They would keep her mind occupied, and stop her from thinking about Mark and Clarissa and their wretched ball tonight.

She was determined to waste no time in getting the stables started. A little later in the day she would drive to Bulawayo and talk to someone at the bank about the account Mark had promised to set up for her. There was the electricity to be connected. Even more important, she had to see about getting a telephone. A few days earlier, in her hotel room in Bulawayo, she had made some preliminary calls to carpenters, plumbers and electricians; now she was ready to get quotes for the work that had to be done.

It was also time to do something about the house itself. Within the limits of what she felt she could spend, Tiffany intended to make her home more attractive. For the stables, she needed contractors. In the house, she could do much of the work herself.

She came back from town early in the afternoon, stopping in surprise as she approached the house. Two people waited for her on the veranda, a woman and a boy of ten or eleven.

'I've come about a job,' said the woman, after Tiffany had greeted her and asked how she could help her. She had a round face and an open, friendly smile. The boy's mother, Tiffany thought, noting the resemblance in the two faces.

'What kind of job?' Tiffany asked.

'Housekeeping.' There was dignity in the woman's bearing, but there was intense anxiety too.

'There's only me here, and I don't really need a housekeeper,' Tiffany said slowly.

The woman looked past at her, at the house. 'This is a big place, and I'm a good housekeeper. My boy, he's strong and willing, he could help around the yard and in the fields.'

'I don't know your name...'

'Betty Mitlusi.'

'And your son?'

'His name is Jonas.'

'Do you go to school, Jonas?' Tiffany asked, turning to the boy.

'Yes, ma'am,' he said, but not very happily, and Tiffany saw the cloud that appeared briefly in his mother's eyes.

'Jonas goes to school,' Betty said. 'It's not far from here. He can work in the afternoons.'

There was something intensely vulnerable and a little sad about the pair. Tiffany felt herself being drawn to them. She wondered how long they had been waiting for her.

'I wouldn't expect a big salary,' Betty said, looking at Tiffany with her big dark eyes. 'Jonas and I need a place to live. The drought has done bad things to our country, and people are hurting.'

And you are hurting too, Tiffany thought. She wondered whether Betty had a husband, whether she and Jonas were in touch with him. She wondered whether they had been on the road long, looking in vain for a job. Questions she did not feel able to ask.

'I'm a good worker,' Betty said.

'I'm sure you are...'

But Tiffany's words as much as her tone implied that there was no job to be had. The other woman understood; she did not need the message spelled out to her. She looked at her son, and he followed her down the steps. Betty held her head high; she was clearly a proud person who would not let her feelings show, but Tiffany thought she saw a hint of tears in the eyes of the boy.

They were beginning to walk down the drive towards the road when Tiffany called after them, 'Wait!'

They turned, and she saw caution in their faces. Quickly she walked down the steps and joined them on the sun-baked ground.

'I'm going to be starting a business here,' she told them. 'Stables. I'll be giving riding lessons and looking after horses for other people.'

'*Horses*?' The boy's eyes sparkled with sudden interest.

Tiffany was intrigued. 'Do you know anything about horses, Jonas?'

'I love them,' he said fervently. 'I love horses more than anything in the world.'

'I love them too.' They smiled at each other in a moment of perfect understanding.

Tiffany turned back to Betty. 'I'm going to be so busy setting up the business that I may not have much time for other things. It would be very nice if you could take care of the house for me. And in the afternoons, after school, Jonas can help me in the stables.'

For a few seconds Betty looked as if she could not believe what she was hearing. 'Thank you,' she said then. 'We will have to fetch our things.'

'Take your time, I'll be glad to see you whenever you're ready.'

'Thank you,' Betty said again. She looked so overcome with happiness and relief that Tiffany felt a lump come to her throat.

She watched Betty and Jonas walk away, the woman solid and dignified, the boy small and shy and so slight that it was difficult to imagine him exerting his will over a stubborn horse. But Tiffany remembered the brilliance in his eyes when she'd said Jonas could help her in the stables, the lift of his head as he'd cast a quick glance at his mother. And she knew, instinctively, that the decision made in a moment of compassion was one she would never regret.

The sun's rays pressed down on the land, and the rockpiles shimmered in a heat haze. It was the hottest time of the day—just a few minutes in the sun, and already Tiffany felt enervated. She walked back up the steps and into the house—and found that it was even hotter indoors than outside. She would have liked nothing more than to spend an hour soaking in a cool bath, but that luxury would have to wait.

The phone company had made her no promises, yet, miracle of miracles, when she lifted the receiver of the instrument which had hitherto been dead, a welcome crackle sounded through the line.

For the next hour Tiffany sat in the kitchen with her notes and drawings spread around her, making calls and arranging appointments. The calendar in front of her acquired a busy look.

The sun was beginning to set when she carried her dinner to the veranda. She put a plate with bread and cheese and a small tossed salad on a table, and pulled up a chair.

The air was quiet and not as hot as it had been. The sunset was dramatic, the sky awash with vivid colours. Looking across the garden and the fields towards the *veld*, Tiffany marvelled anew at the harshness and beauty of the country she had decided to make her home.

The sunset was as brief as it was brilliant. Darkness descended suddenly, quickly, and now the air came alive with the shrilling of the crickets. Tiffany sat back and closed her eyes, only to wince with pain as a picture appeared from nowhere in her mind.

Mark was there, tall and distinguished in an elegant dinner suit. And Clarissa, beautiful and flamboyantly sexy with her shining blonde hair loose and cascading around her shoulders, a flame-red dress moulding itself like another skin to her seductive figure. They were on a dance floor, arms around each other, bodies so close together that the two people could have been one.

'*No*!' Tiffany cried, and clasped her hands tightly over her eyes, as if in that way she could erase the picture. But it remained in her mind.

Agitated now, she rose quickly from her chair and went back to the hot kitchen where she had left some rolls of wallpaper earlier in the day. She measured the walls and cut the paper. Such pretty paper: women in a variety of romantic old-fashioned costumes against a pale amber background. Tiffany had been enchanted with the wallpaper when she'd seen it in the shop in Bulawayo, but she barely looked at the pictures now. Because, as she began to paste the paper to the walls, that other picture remained behind her eyes, refusing to go away.

CHAPTER SEVEN

'YOU missed a bit just here...'

A muscular arm stretched past Tiffany, a tanned hand taking the paintbrush out of her fingers.

'*Mark*!' Tiffany gasped, as she jerked backwards from the fence-post she was painting. 'I had no idea you were here! Why on earth did you creep up on me like that?'

'So engrossed in your thoughts of me that you didn't hear my car?' Mark drawled.

'You're flattering yourself, but then modesty isn't exactly your most outstanding feature, is it?' she shot back. 'As for not hearing you—I guess I was absorbed in my work.'

In fact, her thoughts had been with the man who was now towering above her: painful thoughts about his evening with Clarissa, wondering if she would see him again, wishing she did not care so much. She watched him fill in the small patch of wood she had missed.

'Playing truant from the office?' she asked, as he gave her back her brush.

'I was in court until just over an hour ago.'

After which he must have stopped somewhere to change from his office clothes into the casual jeans and open-necked shirt he wore now. As always, Tiffany found the ease with which he was able to transform himself from elegant lawyer into supple outdoor man fascinating.

'Did you win your case?' she asked curiously.

Dark eyes lit with a satisfied gleam. 'Very thoroughly, I'm happy to say.'

On a burst of intuition, Tiffany said, 'The opposition you trounced—Brent Sawyer?'

'Yes, but let's change the subject, shall we? After a day of Brent's obnoxious courtroom dramatics, I'd be glad to forget the man's existence for a while.'

'You haven't told me why you're here, Mark. Or is this just a routine trip to a client?'

He stood in front of her, overwhelmingly male, with his hands on his hips, and his feet planted firmly on the sand. 'You're not exactly a client, Tiffany,' he said mockingly.

'But you do have the final say over everything I do,' she responded tersely.

'Financially speaking, yes—which is one of the reasons I like to know how you're getting on,' he agreed.

And that was all there was to the visit. The trustee of Andrew's fortune, making sure his money was not going to be squandered by a gold-digging beneficiary. Silly of her to have thought, even for a moment, that there could be any other reason for Mark Rowlands to drive out so far on the weekday afternoon. Bending her head so that he would not see the tell-tale disappointment in her eyes, Tiffany dipped her brush into the pot of white paint.

'You could have saved yourself the effort,' she said brightly. 'I'm getting on very well, as you can see.'

Mark's laughter was low and vibrant and far too close to her ear. 'I do indeed. Do you have a spare brush?'

'Why?'

'I happen to be a dab hand with paint.'

'The lawyer coming out all this way to spruce up a dilapidated old fence?'

'If you want to put it like that.'

'Fine!' She threw him a spirited look. 'As it happens, I do have another brush. You've got yourself a job, Mark—see you do it well. One thing, though—if you expect payment, state your price now. I like to know where I stand at the outset.'

His gaze lingered on her mouth for a long moment, before moving very slowly down her throat to her breasts.

'I don't expect payment in the form of hard currency, Tiffany.'

As his eyes came back to hers, she saw the devilment in them, and knew that she had understood his meaning correctly.

'I don't believe in the barter system,' she managed to say lightly.

'Pity, because I don't want any money.'

'I guess there's no deal in that event. You can get in your car, Mark, and go right back to Bulawayo.'

He chuckled, an oddly intimate sound. 'On second thoughts—why don't you give me that brush anyway?'

Tiffany had left the spare brush and the rest of the paint on the veranda, out of the heat. By the time she returned to the fence she saw that Mark had rolled up his shirt-sleeves to the elbows. He took the brush from her hand, his fingers touching hers, lingering against them quite deliberately. A second passed, and then Tiffany removed her fingers. Mark did not comment, but she saw the glint in the dark eyes in the moment before he dipped his brush in the paint.

Tiffany had thought they would work on different fence-posts, but that, apparently, was not Mark's way. Squatting, his knees just inches from hers, he applied paint to one side of the post while she worked on the other. Working together, she quickly realised, was altogether different from working alone: companionable, fun—and very intimate. Once, when their paintbrushes met at the side of the post, Mark's brush stroked Tiffany's in a languorous motion that reminded her of a sensual caress. Her breathing was suddenly a little shallow.

With one fence-post completed, they moved to the next one, working together in harmony. Tiffany could not help wondering what it would be like to share all her activities with Mark. She knew the answer to that, of course—it would be bliss. She knew too that to let her thoughts drift that way was both futile and dangerous.

It was a while before she allowed herself to ask the question that had been hovering on her tongue since the moment of his arrival.

'Did you have a good time at the ball?'

'Very.'

'Clarissa must have looked stunning in her new dress.'

'Stunning is the word.'

'Sexy too, I suppose?'

Questions she would not have been able to ask if they had been looking at each other, but with her hands occupied and her eyes well concealed beneath her lashes, the words emerged.

'Sexy too,' Mark drawled insolently.

'Clarissa is... She's very beautiful.' It was becoming increasingly difficult for Tiffany to keep her voice casual. With all her heart she wished that she had never embarked on this particular line of conversation.

'Clarissa is beautiful,' Mark agreed drily.

Tiffany's brush-strokes grew faster; her side of the fence-post was beginning to acquire an uneven look.

For a while they worked in silence. It was very quiet in the yard. A slight breeze turned the silver blades of a distant windmill, and ruffled the branches of the bluegums. An army of ants was making its way across the sand, its ranks forming a disciplined line. When a large bird flew suddenly over the yard, its wing-span created a moving shadow over the sun-baked ground.

Mark spoke eventually. 'You are beautiful too, Tiffany,' he said in a new tone.

The breath caught in her throat. 'I am?'

'Don't you know it?' he asked softly.

'No...' Her cheeks had grown warm beneath his gaze.

'Well, you are beautiful, rose nymph. And I want very much to make love to you.'

It was what Tiffany wanted too, more than anything else in the world at that moment, but she knew she would be sorry later if she gave in to the hunger burning inside her.

'There's a fence to finish,' she said unsteadily.

But Mark was not content to leave it at that. 'We could go on with it later. Or even tomorrow.'

Tiffany jerked violently as one of her knees was suddenly captured between his. For a single wild moment she thought it was an accident, that this had happened, somehow, when he moved. One look at his face, at the wickedness of his expression, and she knew that he had acted deliberately.

'*No*!' she said fiercely, yanking away from him.

'I believe you want to make love too, Tiffany.'

'You're wrong, Mark.' Her heart was beating so quickly now that it was an effort to speak with any measure of calm. 'Making love is the last thing on my mind.'

'Lies, rose nymph.'

'No! There's a fence to be painted. If you want to help me, fine. If you'd rather leave, that will be fine too.'

His eyebrows lifted in an expression that was both cynical and amused, his grin making his teeth look dangerous against his tan.

'That's really what you want?'

'Absolutely,' she answered him grimly.

They went on working, silently once more, far too close together for Tiffany's comfort. She was so acutely aware of Mark that she quivered with tension. She could only hope that he did not see it.

'Tell me about him,' he said after a while.

Tiffany looked at him, puzzled. 'Andrew?'

'If he was the man in your life.'

'I've told you several times that he wasn't. Why can't you believe that?'

'Perhaps I'm beginning to,' Mark surprised her by saying. He paused just a moment. 'If not Andrew, there was someone else.'

Tiffany grew very still. A few drops of paint fell to the ground from the brush suspended in her hand. 'Why do you say that?'

'Because you're too beautiful a woman not to have had a man in your life.'

'Mark...' she began, guessing the direction he was taking, desperate to head him off.

Perceptive eyes raked her face in a look that reminded Tiffany that Mark Rowlands was an expert at judging people, at comprehending the meanings that lay beneath the shallow surface of words. She regarded him unhappily, knowing that nothing she could say would deter him from speaking his thoughts.

'And because there has to be a reason why you stiffen every time I want to make love to you,' he added.

'You're guessing,' Tiffany said tersely.

'But I'm right, am I not?' He sounded so confident that the words barely constituted a question.

Tiffany did not answer.

He caught her chin in his free hand. 'Tell me about him.'

Their eyes held for what seemed like an interminable moment. And then Tiffany was pulling away from him and turning her attention to the fence-post once more. Her brush-strokes were more erratic than ever now. When the paint was dry she would have to scrape it all off and start again. But she had no intention of stopping: if she was going to talk—and Mark seemed determined that she should—it would be easier this way.

'His name was Wayde,' she said at last, her voice so low that Mark had strain to hear it.

'Wayde?'

'Wayde Thompson. We were so much in love. At least, I thought we were in love.'

'He didn't want to make a commitment?'

'He met someone else. His boss's daughter, his only child. Wayde saw a way of advancing himself. It's an old story, really.'

'Except that in this case it's *your* story, and that's what makes it painful.' Mark spoke gently, with an understanding Tiffany had not expected from him.

'Yes...'

'You broke up, I suppose.'

'That happens all the time too. Except that it happened two days before we were to have been married. With the wedding-dress hanging in the wardrobe, the cake in the very last stages of decoration, and gifts piling up in the spare room of an aunt's house.'

Mark made a sound in his throat. 'That must have been rough.'

Tiffany looked at him, her lips trembling, her eyes distraught. 'I never guessed that Wayde and Barbara were anything but friends. When Wayde told me the wedding was off, I was certain he was joking, I thought he was just putting me through a test of some kind. I was devastated when I realised that he was really serious about ending our relationship. They were married within the month. When they returned from their honeymoon, Wayde was given a huge promotion, and he's been climbing the business ladder ever since. When Barbara's father retires he'll take over completely.'

'Are you still in love with him?' Mark's eyes were peculiarly alert, but Tiffany was too shaken to notice.

'I haven't been for a long time. Wayde means nothing to me any more.'

'But he's made you scared to trust other men?'

Tiffany hesitated a moment. For so long she had tried to empty her mind of memories: the wedding-dress which she had boxed and sent to a friend who was getting married and was hard pressed to afford a dress of her own, the gifts which she had sent back to their donors accompanied by apologetic explanatory notes, the cake which she had thrown out with the rubbish. And the worst memory of all: passing the church just as Wayde and Barbara, covered with confetti, were walking to the bridal car.

Since that day, Tiffany had barely mentioned Wayde's name. Yet, curiously, the telling of the story was not as traumatic as it might have been. Mark's closeness had a lot to do with that, she understood. Also the fact that if she had ever wondered whether any unrequited feelings for Wayde remained, that fear had been soundly laid to rest.

As for trust, that was something else...

'I don't want to be hurt again,' she said slowly. 'I was lucky in one sense—it wasn't long after the break-up that I met Andrew. To begin with, he was only my employer, but he quickly became so much more. You keep asking me if we were lovers. It was never like that—though we did love each other deeply. Andrew was like an uncle...the father I'd lost before I met him. With Andrew I was never frightened, I knew he wouldn't hurt me.'

'Not all men are like Wayde,' Mark said flatly.

'Maybe not. But then I wouldn't have thought Wayde was capable of behaving the way he did.' She searched the autocratic face for some glimmer of understanding, and saw only hardness instead.

Perhaps it had been a mistake to confide in Mark after all. It did not matter that he was the man she loved: he was also a stranger, an adversary, a person devoid of compassion. Especially where she was concerned. 'I hope you can understand now why I have to protect myself,' she said grimly. 'Sex isn't for me, Mark. It can't be.'

'Even though your body craves it? Because I know it does, Tiffany. You're a woman of deep passion, I've sensed it every time I've touched you.'

It was galling to realise how completely he understood her.

'Even then,' Tiffany whispered, her cheeks flaming as she realised the admission she'd made.

They went on painting, but now Tiffany left Mark at one fence-post while she went on to another. As if he sensed her inner tension, he made no move to join her. For a while they worked in silence once more, then Mark began to talk.

Easy talk, about a case he was working on, the different personalities involved, the problems. Slowly, Tiffany began to relax. She enjoyed hearing him talk. She had told him the truth when she'd said that Wayde meant nothing to her any more—it was only reliving the hurt that was so upsetting. Mark was the man who engaged her mind now, as well as her emotions.

The fence was long. Together they moved from post to post. When Mark had finished telling Tiffany about the court case, she told him about the couple she'd engaged to work for her: the dignified woman, Betty, and Jonas, her son. And she told him about her discussions with the contractors.

'What will you call the place?' he asked.

Tiffany lifted her head. 'Isn't it odd, I hadn't thought about that? I suppose I should come up with a name.'

'If it's going to be a business, yes.'

Tiffany was not quiet for more than a few minutes. When she spoke again, she was smiling. 'There really is only one name.'

'And that is?'

'Donaldson's Place.'

'It doesn't belong to Andrew any longer.'

'But it did. Besides, Donaldson's Place was the name of his stables in England.'

'I didn't know that. Why not think of something new, Tiffany?'

'It doesn't seem right to do that. I owe so much to Andrew; I believe he'd have been happy to know his name would continue.'

'Donaldson's Place it is, then?' Mark's expression was enigmatic.

'Yes,' she said.

'Will you be advertising the stables, Tiffany?'

'I think I should, don't you? And quite soon. The barn will be ready for use by next week.' Tiffany looked at Mark, her eyes at once eager and uncertain. 'Now that I'm so close to it, I'm praying things will work out.'

Dark eyes lingered broodingly on her face, so intently that Tiffany wished she knew what Mark was thinking.

'I have a feeling things will work out very well,' he said then, and she sensed that he was talking about something other than the stables.

It was only when Mark said, 'Not much painting light left today,' that Tiffany realised how dark it had been getting. Mark helped her clean the brushes and close up the tins of paint. They were walking back towards the house when she invited him to stay for supper.

He grinned. 'Thought you'd never get round to it.'

'Nothing fancy,' she warned him. 'My provisions at the moment don't run to much more than hamburgers and a few ingredients for a salad.'

'With a good Riesling, the meal will be perfect.'

'I don't have any wine, Mark.'

'Isn't it lucky, in that case, that I do?'

Tiffany couldn't help laughing. 'You knew all the time I'd invite you?'

'No—but I intended hanging around till you did.'

She lifted her chin at him. 'Do you always get what you want?'

'Eventually,' he assured her wickedly.

It was so hot in the kitchen that they decided to barbecue the meat out of doors. While Tiffany made a salad and cut up some bread, Mark built a fire in a brick pit near the house. When the flames had died low he laid the hamburgers on the grid. By the time the meat was ready the sun had vanished beneath the horizon. They ate their meal by the fire, their only light coming from the flickering flames and from a candle perched on a low table between them.

It was a companionable meal—they talked and laughed easily. Watching the candlelight play on Mark's face, shadowing his eyes, accenting the hollows beneath his cheekbones, softening the tough line of his jaw, Tiffany knew that in all her life she had never enjoyed the company of a more attractive man.

The flames had died to nothing when he said, 'Finding the bed comfortable?'

Tiffany stiffened. 'Why do you ask?'

'I'm interested. Do you?'

She shifted in her chair. 'It's a nice bed.'

'You haven't answered the question.'

'I thought I did.'

'Liar—you know that you did not.' His laughter was low and mocking in the scented darkness. 'It doesn't take a lawyer to understand that you're prevaricating. You haven't slept in the bed, have you, Tiffany?'

'Maybe not...'

'Why? Are you a martyr, that you prefer a cold stone floor to the comfort of a good mattress?'

'Don't be silly,' she muttered.

'If that's silly, then maybe it's the fact that *I* gave you the bed that's keeping you out of it?'

Tiffany remained silent.

'Which is it?' Mark persisted.

'I don't have to answer your questions,' she said tartly. 'You're not in court now, and I'm not in the witness box.'

Mark laughed. 'True.' His voice changed, his tone becoming huskily seductive. 'You don't have to answer this question either, but perhaps you'd like to know what I was thinking about last night?'

'Since you were at the ball together, something about Clarissa, no doubt.' Tiffany kept her voice light.

'Later.'

Had there been a time during the night when Mark had been alone? Tiffany wished the answer to that question did not matter to her quite so much.

'I was picturing you in the bed.' His tone was even more seductive now, nerve-tinglingly so. 'I saw you lying there alone—when I should have been with you, making love to you. Wild, passionate love, Tiffany.'

'Don't!' she protested in a choked voice.

'I pictured you in those sexy bits of nothing I found you wearing the morning I surprised you in your sleeping-bag.'

'Stop this, Mark! Don't you realise you're upsetting me?'

But as if he did not hear a word she said, Mark continued, 'Do you ever sleep in the nude, Tiffany?'

'It's none of your damn business what I do!'

'I want to see you in the bed, Tiffany.'

'No!' she protested wildly.

'Yes,' he insisted.

She jumped from her chair and tried to get away from him, but he was quicker than she was. He was coming towards her, and as she turned to look at him, she found the wall of the house at her back. The tall male body was in front of her, around her, blocking her means of escape.

He reached for her, lifting her in his arms, carrying her into the house as easily as if she were weightless. Through the dark passage he carried her, into the bedroom, where he flicked on the light. Still holding her, he bent, picked up the sleeping-bag, unzipped it and spread it over the bed. Then he put her down on it.

Tiffany sat up immediately. She was about to get off the bed, when Mark gripped her shoulders and said, 'Please, don't...'

There was a huskiness in his tone which she had not heard before. A vulnerability which she had never suspected, and which reached to the very core of her being.

'Stay there,' Mark said, and knelt beside her.

'I can't...'

'Don't be frightened. I would never force myself on you, Tiffany, never hurt you. Don't you know that, sweetheart? All I want is to see your naked body. To kiss you and touch you and make love to you. I want you to admit to yourself that you want it as much as I do.'

He began to lace her hair through his fingers, drawing it tighter and tighter until her head was lifted from the bed and drawn to his. She flinched as his tongue traced a path around her lips, setting off a torrent of fire deep inside her.

'*No*!' She was trembling violently as she twisted away from him. 'Stop this, Mark! You have to stop!'

'Don't fight the inevitable, Tiffany,' he whispered into her mouth. 'You can't deny that we've been attracted to each other from the moment we met. What's happening now was written in the stars.'

'But you don't trust me, Mark,' she protested despairingly. 'You still think of me as a schemer.'

'It doesn't stop me from wanting you.'

With the knowledge that he would never change his mind about her, she should have been able to fight him. He had said that he would not force himself on her, and instinctively she believed him. But in order to fight him she first had to fight herself, and that was unbelievably difficult. When he began to kiss her, it became impossible.

One kiss followed another, and Tiffany lost all will to fight or to escape. Drugging kisses that robbed her of all rational thought. Kisses that were at first achingly sweet, that hardened, becoming wild and throbbing. As one kiss merged into another, tremor after tremor shook Tiffany's body. Before she knew it, she was reciprocating with an abandon she had never suspected was in her.

She did nothing to stop Mark when he tugged at her buttons and pushed her blouse from her shoulders, when his hands went to her back to open the clasp of her bra; when he slid her jeans down over her hips she lifted herself from the sleeping-bag to make his task easier. She did not stop him when his hands went to her breasts, his fingers exploring the nipples that firmed and hardened in response to his touch. And then he was lying down beside her, gathering her to him, and his hands were exploring her body with a greater intimacy than ever before—moving over her throat, her breasts, her buttocks, kindling her senses to wildfire with lips and tongue on her throat, over the swell of her breasts, closing over her nipples. And her hands were on him too, shaping themselves to the hard bones of his shoulders and back and hips, fingers tightening in the hair at the back of his neck and chest, caressing his throat and chest. And a thought clamoured in her head—how could she not have known that lovemaking could be so beautiful?

Mark moved against her, and as she became aware of the pulsing hardness of his body she moved blindly against him. She needed to be part of him, one with him in the way that she had never experienced.

She gave a little moan as he lifted himself away from her. And then she saw that he was unbuckling his belt. A thought came to her. Something she had to tell him, share with him. It made no difference to what was going to happen—she had no intention of drawing back now, she needed him to give her fulfilment—but it was something he had to know all the same.

He was drawing her to him once more when she said, 'Mark...'

'Yes, sweetheart...'

'I'm a virgin.'

He looked down at her, his expression one of utter astonishment. 'There was Wayde.'

'I never let him make love to me.'

'I didn't know... Didn't guess... That makes this doubly special.'

'I had to tell you.'

'I won't hurt you, Tiffany.'

She knew that, and she was not frightened.

'It's just...' she began in a whisper. 'I...I'm not protected.'

Mark laughed softly. 'That isn't a problem. I have something with me.'

At the last words, Tiffany stiffened. She felt cold suddenly. Mark tried to draw her back into his arms, but she made herself even more rigid.

'What is it?' he wanted to know.

She was very close to tears. 'I can't go on with this.'

'You knew what was going to happen,' he said disbelievingly. 'Even if you are a virgin, you must have known, and you made no effort to stop me.'

'Yes...'

'What is this all about, Tiffany? You've chosen a hell of a moment to go cold on me.' This was the contemptuous Mark, his voice hard and harsh.

Tiffany was angry all at once. 'You're accusing me, Mark Rowlands? That's beautiful!'

'Mind telling me why you're so upset?'

Pushing herself away from him, Tiffany sat up, found her blouse and tugged it roughly over her shoulders. Her fingers were too taut to do up the buttons, but she managed to hold the sides of the blouse over her breasts.

'You knew all the time that this was going to happen,' she said.

'I hoped it would.'

'You came prepared. Wine to act as an aphrodisiac, and afterwards, when I'd be panting for you to make love to me, protection.'

'So what?'

Bitterness clogged her throat. 'You'd made up your mind before you left Bulawayo that you were going to seduce me.'

'I don't understand your outrage. Would it have been better if I'd arrived unprepared?' Mark's voice was laced with hard contempt. 'A night of passion—and an unwanted pregnancy to worry about afterwards. Don't you think that would have been a lot worse?'

When he had left the dance with Clarissa last night, had Mark been similarly prepared then too? How many other women had there been in the past? How many were there now? And could Tiffany endure being just one more woman in his life?

She shook her head, unable to tell him why she felt so repulsed.

'What you're saying makes perfect sense,' she said miserably, 'but it's too calculated, too impersonal. It makes me realise that this isn't for me after all.'

Mark's mouth was hard, his eyes bleak. 'Why won't you give yourself a chance, Tiffany?'

'It's impossible.'

'Because of Wayde? Because there's a part of you that still loves him? Or because you're frightened of being hurt?'

Tiffany was frightened, she knew that. The parting from Wayde had hurt at the time, but eventually she had got over it. Making love with Mark would be the most wonderful experience of her life. But when he left her, as she knew he would, she would never recover from the pain.

With an effort, she said, 'Because I'm not ready for this.'

'When will you be ready?'

The eyes that met his were smudged with unhappiness and unrequited passion. 'Maybe never,' Tiffany said.

CHAPTER EIGHT

IT SEEMED to Tiffany sometimes as if Betty and Jonas had always been with her. They fitted in quite naturally, their presence easy and pleasant. Until the business began to show a profit, Tiffany would have to budget her money carefully, yet she had never regretted employing the mother and her son. After just a short while, they had begun to make themselves indispensable.

Responding to Betty's loving attention to detail, the house looked more attractive every day. Her expertise in the kitchen was no less impressive—the meals she produced were so irresistible that a laughing Tiffany predicted that she would find herself having to buy a new wardrobe before long.

Jonas was a sparkling, fun-loving boy. He spent his weekday mornings at school, but it was clear that the classroom was not the place he liked best. Tiffany would see him sometimes leaving for school in the mornings, shoulders drooping, expression woebegone, quite unlike the boy who returned in the afternoons, vital, alive, always in search of something to do.

He was never happier than when Tiffany found him a challenging task in the yard or the developing stables. He possessed a quick and unerring hand with a hammer and a screwdriver; there was not a chore around the place which Jonas could not perform. But his passion was horses. He talked about them constantly, begging Tiffany to let him take over the grooming and care of any horse she acquired.

One afternoon Tiffany was in the yard, refurbishing some old saddles she had found at an auction. Her hands were oily with polish when she realised that she had not read the instructions completely. She was looking around in vain for something to wipe her hands on, when Jonas walked into the yard.

'Hello there!' she called out happily. 'Just the person I wanted to see.'

'Hello, Tiffany.' Both Betty and her son had started off by calling Tiffany 'ma'am', but she had quickly told them that the title made her uncomfortable, and had insisted they call her by her first name instead.

'I was in too much of a hurry to get started, and now I've run into a problem—will you read me the instructions, please, Jonas?'

The boy's smile vanished. Tiffany, glancing ruefully at her oily hands, did not notice the change in his expression.

'Look, Jonas, there's the paper—on the ground by the tin.'

Still Jonas did not move. Tiffany looked at him, puzzled.

'I'd read the instructions myself, but my hands are a mess and I don't want to dirty the paper. I can't go on until I know what to do. Please, read to me, Jonas.'

The boy stepped reluctantly forward, took the leaflet from the ground, and looked at it. His fingers clutched the paper tightly, his eyes stared at it, his lips moved, as if forming sounds—but no sound came.

'Jonas...?' Tiffany said, very gently now.

He looked up. His face was tense, his eyes stark with unhappiness. The leaflet dropped from his hands, and he made no effort to retrieve it. For a second longer he stared at Tiffany. Then he wheeled, and ran out of the yard.

Much later, when she knew that Jonas would have gone to his room, Tiffany confronted Betty in the kitchen.

'Tell me about Jonas.'

Betty, who was busy drying dishes, hesitated. Tiffany had been aware of her tension all evening. She sat down at the round kitchen table, pulled out a second chair, and beckoned to the housekeeper.

'Sit down with me, Betty.'

Still the woman hesitated.

'Please, Betty—you know we have to talk.'

Slowly, unhappily, Betty put the dish on the counter, wiped her hands on a towel, and sat down.

'Jonas has trouble reading?' Tiffany asked quietly.

Betty's eyes were averted. 'Yes.'

'Can he read at all?'

'Not really.'

'Nothing?'

'A little. Very little. Like a small child. I . . . I've tried to help him . . .'

'But he can't get it right?'

'It's all a jumble. He reads words backwards, upside down.' Betty was still unable to meet Tiffany's eyes.

'Does he have trouble with letters like D and B? Does he get them mixed up?'

The housekeeper nodded. 'All the time.'

Tiffany leaned forward in her chair. 'Why didn't you tell me?'

'I . . . I couldn't.'

'It's obvious you know what happened this afternoon. If I hadn't asked Jonas to read to me, I'd never have guessed he had a problem. He's a lovely boy, and so intelligent.'

'*Intelligent*!' From the expression on Betty's face it was clear that she thought Tiffany was crazy.

'Yes, Betty, intelligent. I see his skills all the time. There's so much that Jonas can do. Tell him something once, and he understands right away. I can't tell you how happy I am to have him around.'

Betty was silent.

'He just has a reading problem,' Tiffany said. 'It's nothing to be ashamed of, you know.'

'But he is ashamed, and it's getting worse all the time. The kids at school, they make fun of him. What will he do when he grows up? A man who can't read?' Betty spread her hands in despair.

'If I'm not mistaken, Jonas has a problem called dyslexia,' Tiffany said quietly. 'Other people have that problem too. Many do.'

'Really?' It was clear from Betty's expression that she was convinced her son's difficulties were unique.

'I had a good friend who couldn't read, but in every other way he was a clever, competent man. Jonas can be helped, Betty.'

The housekeeper looked at her disbelievingly. 'At the farm school there are so many children. The teachers try hard, but they are busy...'

Tiffany's eyes turned inwards. She saw another boy, isolated, unhappy, so concerned about the reactions of his family and his friends to a problem he had not been able to conquer that he'd felt compelled to leave his home and make a new life for himself elsewhere.

'I may be able to help Jonas,' she said.

The housekeeper looked astonished. 'Are you a teacher, Tiffany?'

'Not that kind of teacher. But I've spent a lot of time learning about reading problems, and I believe I may be able to do something for Jonas. At least a little. He'd need a special teacher as well, but maybe I could give him some confidence.'

'You would do that?' Betty was looking at her with glowing eyes. 'I can't afford very much...'

'I wouldn't take any money from you, Betty.'

'Then why...?'

'I'd be doing it because I'm fond of Jonas.' Tiffany paused a moment before adding, 'And because someone I once knew would be happy to know that I'd helped.'

Two days later, Tiffany had things to do in the city. When she had been to the bank and purchased things for the stables, she stopped first at a library, then at a bookshop. In the library she found a book that she wanted, in the shop two others. She also bought a pack of index cards and some brightly coloured pens and pencils.

After supper that evening, she sat by the lamp in the living-room and began to read. Fascinated with the different aspects of dyslexia and the ways in which they could be remedied, she did not notice the passing of the hours. It was only when the words began to blur before her eyes that she glanced at her watch and saw that it was well past midnight.

Next day, when Jonas returned from school, Tiffany sat down with him and organised a lesson plan. For two hours after supper every evening they would study together, and several more hours at the weekend.

She spoke with Betty as well. Together they would visit the school, and set about finding a teacher who could help Jonas.

'You'll read as well as anyone in your class,' she promised the boy.

A few days later, Tiffany had a visitor. She was glancing through a farming magazine on the veranda when she heard the sound of a car coming up the drive.

Mark? she wondered, with an involuntary leaping of the senses. She had not laid eyes on him since the day he had walked out of her bedroom. When a week had gone by without a word from him, Tiffany had tried to convince herself that his absence was for the good. Yet knowing that she was better off without him did not lessen the almost physical ache with which she missed him.

But the car that came into view was unfamiliar. Puzzled, Tiffany watched it draw up near the front of the house. It was a sporty model, bright red and more than a little showy. And then the door opened and the driver got out, and she recognised him immediately.

'Brent Sawyer...' A smile hid her disappointment as she met him at the top of the steps. 'This *is* a surprise!'

'A pleasant one, I hope?' He took her hand and kissed it, as he'd done the first time they had met. 'Not intruding, I hope, lovely lady?'

'Of course not, it's nice to see you again.'

Blue eyes sparkled with malicious laughter. 'Kind of you to say so.'

She laughed with him. 'Kind?'

She watched him as he looked around. He was dressed in sleek white pants and a bright yellow shirt, with two gold chains adorning his throat. Where Mark Rowlands was all rugged toughness, Brent Sawyer was unashamedly flamboyant. His type was one that would never appeal to Tiffany on a physical level, yet she was just lonely enough to respond to his blatant flirtatiousness. Fortunately, it was obvious that he did not expect her to take him seriously.

'Very nice,' he said.

'It's coming on, thank you. Why are you here, Brent?'

'To feast my eyes on your exquisite appearance.'

'Exquisite?' Tiffany glanced down at her T-shirt and jeans. Good thing Mark was not here, she thought: Brent's particular brand of flattery would make Mark seethe. Still, she could not help being amused by the man's nonsense.

'I have some iced tea in the refrigerator,' she said drily. 'Why don't you sit down while I get us each a glass? Then you can tell me why you're really here.'

When Brent had lavished extravagant praise on the rather ordinary refreshments, Tiffany brought him back to the reason for his visit.

He made a rueful face. 'So you don't believe that I am here merely to see you?'

'You don't really expect me to.'

'I'm mortally wounded.' For a moment, his eyes took on a mournful look. Then his lips lifted at the corners. 'Fortunately, there is one other reason for my visit.'

'Now we're getting to it.'

'I have a horse, beautiful lady. I wonder if you'd be interested in stabling him for me?'

Tiffany sat forward in her chair, her eyes sparkling with sudden excitement. 'My first customer!'

'The very first? Really? That has to herald well for our future relationship.'

'We don't have a relationship, Brent,' Tiffany said firmly. 'Let's talk about your horse.'

They spent the next hour talking about the stables and the facilities Tiffany was able to offer: about grooming and exercise and feed.

'What are your charges?' Brent wanted to know.

Tiffany gave him a figure, and waited anxiously for his reaction. But Brent accepted the figure with equanimity.

'Why did you come to me?' she asked curiously.

'Why, lovely lady? I need a stable for my horse, I knew you were about to open your doors to the public. Supply and demand. As simple as that.'

'That's all there is to it?'

Brent shrugged, and Tiffany saw once more the spark of malice in his eyes. 'What else could there be?'

What else indeed? A red flag to Mark's temper? A thorn in the tough side of the man who had whipped him in court recently, and who, quite obviously, had never kept his disdain of the other lawyer a secret?

Tiffany decided not to tax Brent with her suspicions. She needed customers; it would be as well to give him the benefit of the doubt.

Arrangements finalised, Brent rose to go. They were at his car when he said, 'Have dinner with me tonight.'

'No... But thank you.'

'Tomorrow night?'

'I don't think so, Brent.'

'Beautiful lady, don't you see that your refusal cuts me to the heart?'

'I see nothing of the kind.' She grinned at him. 'You're an outrageous flirt, Brent Sawyer. What would you do if a woman really thought you meant all those compliments?'

'I would be delighted.'

'And I think you'd get the fright of your life. Have you ever taken any woman seriously?'

He pretended to think about that. 'There's always a first time.'

Tiffany burst out laughing. 'Thanks for the invitation anyway.'

Brent opened the door. With one foot in the car, he said, 'I'm interested—why do you refuse me? Is it Mark?'

She noticed that the teasing light had left his eyes. He was watching her shrewdly now.

'Is Mark the reason, Tiffany?'

'Does there have to be a reason?' she evaded lightly. 'You'll bring me your horse and I'll look after it. Isn't that enough?'

He looked at her a moment longer. Then he reached for her hand once more, kissed the palm lingeringly, and said, 'The invitation remains open. Promise me you'll think about it.'

'I'll do that,' she said.

Watching him drive away, Tiffany asked herself if she had been silly to refuse him. In his superficial way, Brent Sawyer would have given her an entertaining time. An evening out with him would have relieved her loneliness.

It made no sense that she should feel so reluctant to go out with any man but Mark, the one man with whom she could never have a future. But there it was—some things were difficult to justify, one of them being that the thought of an evening with anyone but Mark was less appealing than remaining alone.

'Rose nymph?'

'Why, Mark...' Tiffany's heart leaped as the vital voice sounded through the telephone line.

'Thought I'd phone and see how you're getting on.'

He sounded upbeat and relaxed. As if he'd long forgotten what had happened the last time they'd been together. As if it had meant nothing to him, Tiffany thought on a wave of pain.

'I'm fine,' she told him brightly. 'A little more settled every day. The barn is all prepared for horses, and the new stables are coming on well too. In fact, I'm about ready to buy my first horse.'

'You've decided on an animal?'

'Not yet, but I have two or three in mind. One in particular.'

'Care to look at it together?'

Tiffany gripped the receiver tightly. 'Is this my trustee talking?'

'Why do you ask?'

'I guess you're concerned that I'll waste Andrew's money.'

'If you're wondering whether you need my permission to buy a particular animal—you don't.'

A little disbelievingly, Tiffany said, 'Do you mean you want to come along for the fun of it?'

'Is that so strange?' he drawled.

Actually, it was the last thing she'd expected, which was why she hesitated over her answer. There was a part of her that wanted to say, I'm managing quite well without you, let's keep it that way.

But there was that other part too. Her first horse... It scared Tiffany to know quite how much she wanted Mark to be with her when she bought it.

'Why don't you come with me?' she said lightly.

He arrived early on Saturday morning. Tiffany had just reached the end of a lesson with Jonas. It would be a long while before the boy could read properly, and she was well aware that he needed a teacher with far more expertise than her own, yet in just a short time Jonas had begun to acquire some confidence. For the first time he actually believed that he would read some day, and that fact alone gave Tiffany enormous satisfaction.

Seeing Mark's car coming up the drive, she put the books away quickly. Much as she would have liked to tell him about Jonas, she knew that to do so could lead to an unintentional remark about Andrew, and that would never do.

She opened the door. Mark looked down at her, tall and rugged and dynamically attractive. 'Hello, rose nymph,' he said.

'Hello,' she answered, over a dry throat.

'I brought you something.' He handed her a parcel that was oblong and gift-wrapped.

'What is it?' she asked curiously.

'Take a look.'

She took it from him, opened the wrapping, and ran a finger over a wooden sign with the name 'Donaldson's Place' emblazoned on it. In one corner was a picture of a horse, forelegs lifted; in another, a horseshoe.

'This is wonderful!' Her eyes shone as she looked up at Mark. 'Thank you so much!'

A little muscle seemed to move in his throat. 'When your prospective clients arrive at your gates, they'll know they've come to the right place.'

'They will indeed.'

Tiffany was about to tell him that she had one client already, but at that moment Mark said, 'I left the engine running. Shall we go?' He took her hand as they walked to the car, and as his fingers laced through hers all thoughts of Brent Sawyer left her mind.

One breeder, more than any other, had captured Tiffany's interest at the fair. She had phoned him several times since then, following up the calls with visits to his farm. He had a few horses which she liked, one in particular which she kept going back to.

'So this is Calypso,' Mark said, as they stood together by the paddock fence, watching a horse with a sleek coat and a white diamond patch on its nose.

The horse was, in fact, everything Tiffany had been looking for. Lively enough for her own riding enjoyment, yet gentle and reliable with children. Strong, sturdy and quite beautiful. Jonas would love this horse, Tiffany knew. Already, she could see him lavishing all his attention on it.

'I think Calypso is my horse,' she said.

Mark stood to one side as Tiffany spoke to the breeder, making no attempt to interrupt or influence their discussion. There was some talk about the price of the horse: the breeder reduced his asking figure somewhat, Tiffany increased the amount she was prepared to pay. The deal was concluded and it was arranged that Calypso would be delivered to Donaldson's Place the next day. An excited Tiffany gave her new horse a carrot and a hug.

They were in the car once more when Mark said, 'Congratulations.'

With a forefinger he traced a light path around Tiffany's eyes and around her lips. And then he leaned across the seat, drew her to him, and kissed her.

When he lifted his head, Tiffany looked at him wordlessly. For a long moment their eyes met and held, and Tiffany had the strangest feeling that they were communicating with each other on a level other than the verbal one.

And then Mark slid back into his seat and started the engine.

He took her for lunch to a restaurant that was part of a renovated farmhouse, about twenty miles further down the road. There they sat on a veranda with a slastoed floor and crisp cane furniture and succulent plants in large clay pots.

Mark suggested that Tiffany go for shoulder of lamb, which was the speciality of the house. After he had ordered the same dish for himself, he asked the waiter for a bottle of wine.

'To Tiffany and her stables,' he said, raising his glass to her when the wine had been poured. 'And to Calypso, first horse of many.'

'And to Andrew's memory,' Tiffany added quietly. 'Without whom none of this would have been possible.'

'To Andrew,' Mark said, and she saw his eyes rest thoughtfully on her face.

The food, when it arrived, confirmed the wisdom of Mark's choice: the lamb was beautifully tender, its flavour enhanced by an unusual blending of herbs, and the potatoes and other vegetables that accompanied it were delicious. For a while, Tiffany gave herself over to the enjoyment of the meal, the wine, and Mark's company.

They were starting their dessert when she said, 'I was thinking, I'd like to meet Andrew's relatives.'

Mark's head lifted, his expression was surprised. 'Oh?'

'My meetings with Clarissa haven't gone well——' here she paused for a moment to look at him '—but I'd really like to get to know the rest of the family.'

'What exactly do you have in mind?'

'A party. An early evening barbecue would be nice, I think.'

'Are you sure you want to do this?' There was an odd wariness in Mark's eyes.

'Quite sure.'

'The timing may not be as good as you think it is, Tiffany.'

'I don't see how it could be better. With the house clean and the business about to get on its feet, I can start thinking about other things as well now.'

'You might want to wait until——'

'No more waiting,' she interrupted him. 'I want to do this now.'

'Tiffany...' The odd wariness was still in his eyes.

'What is it, Mark? Andrew's family can't still be upset about his will?'

'You don't think that's possible?'

'I was hoping they'd have forgotten about it by now. And if they haven't, all the more reason to get together. To talk about things... I could tell them about Andrew, about his life in England. I want to get to know them, Mark.'

'You know one member of the family already.'

'Clarissa. They can't all be like her, she has to be one of a kind.' Tiffany's cheeks were flushed suddenly. 'I'll invite her too, of course.'

'She may not accept.'

'That will be up to her to decide. But I so badly want to meet the rest of them. I feel as if I've already waited far too long as it is. My mind is made up, Mark; there will be a barbecue at my house, two weeks from today. Please give me the names and addresses of the people I should invite.'

He treated her to a long, level look. Then he said, 'Very well.' Taking a notebook and pen from his pocket, he began to write.

It was quite late in the afternoon when Mark drove Tiffany back to the house. When he stopped the car, she did not open her door right away, but sat still a few moments, enjoying the sight of her new home: the light shining in the kitchen window, the gloss on the newly-oiled front door, the jays pecking in the bird feeder near the veranda. The place had a lived-in look which had been missing the first few times Tiffany had seen it.

As if he'd read her thoughts, Mark said, 'One more touch to make it complete.'

Tiffany turned to him. 'I'll ask Jonas to hang the sign in the morning.'

'I'll hang it myself now,' Mark said.

They found Jonas knocking nails into a loose fence-post in the yard. He handed over his hammer and a few nails, and then Tiffany and Mark walked down the long driveway to the gates, beside which stood a high post. In no time, Mark had put up the sign.

'Donaldson's Place—officially open for business.' Tiffany heard the laughter in his voice.

Happily, she said, 'I should have people beating a path to my door after this.' She paused uncomfortably as a thought came to her.

More quietly, she added, 'Actually...I already have my first client.'

'You do?' Mark looked surprised. 'Who?'

'A man who wants me to look after his horse.' Her feet shifted restlessly on the sandy ground. 'You might as well know, Mark... It's Brent Sawyer.'

'*Sawyer*!' The name burst from Mark's lips in an explosion of disgust.

'Yes...'

Mark took a step backwards, as if he found Tiffany's nearness suddenly repulsive. 'Why didn't you tell me this earlier?'

'I meant to...'

'What were you trying to hide from me?'

'Nothing,' she said unhappily.

'In all the time we spent together today, you couldn't find a few moments to tell me about Sawyer?' This was Mark Rowlands at his most autocratic, the courtroom lawyer intimidating a witness.

'I didn't keep the news from you on purpose,' Tiffany said tautly. 'I was going to talk to you about Brent when you arrived. And then you gave me the sign, and we left to look at the horses, and somehow... I guess I forgot about Brent. Until a few seconds ago I never gave him another thought.'

She looked up at him. Even in the gathering dusk, she could see the hard set of his mouth, the rigidity of his wide shoulders.

'You don't believe me, Mark.'

'Should I?' he asked grimly.

'I'm getting very tired of having my honesty questioned.'

'I wouldn't question it if you didn't give me reason to, Tiffany.'

Bitterness flooded her, red-hot and deep. What a fool she had been to allow herself to enjoy the day with Mark. After all this time she should have known better than to let down her guard with him.

Furiously, she said, 'We talk and laugh, you kiss me, you pretend to find me desirable, and all the time——'

'Pretend?' he asked, with odd emphasis.

'Pretend,' she echoed blindly. 'And none of it means anything because you don't trust me. First it was Andrew, now it's Brent.'

'Finished?' he asked coldly. 'Because if you are, it's my turn to speak. You talk about trust. I find it very hard to understand that you'd neglect to tell me about your first client—*your first client, Tiffany*.'

'I did tell you.'

'Only now. If I'd known this morning...'

He did not finish the sentence; he didn't have to. His meaning could not have been clearer to Tiffany. Had Mark known about Brent, they would never have spent the day together.

'Brent Sawyer, the one man you know I detest, and you *forget* to mention him to me.' Mark's voice was heavy with contempt.

'Exactly,' Tiffany said defiantly. 'I forgot.'

'Weren't you surprised when Sawyer came to you?'

Tiffany remembered her earlier suspicions, but she wouldn't give Mark the satisfaction of admitting to them. Coolly, she said, 'Should I have been?'

'The stables haven't been advertised. Until a few minutes ago there wasn't even a name on the gates. So why would Brent Sawyer come to you, Tiffany, when there are so many other places to choose from? This isn't the first time he's stabled his horse. *Why you, Tiffany*?'

'He wanted a decent place to keep his animal.'

'You're naïve if you think that's all there is to it. Brent Sawyer and I have a long history of conflict. He knows that you and I...' Mark stopped.

'That you and I—what?' she asked, hiding her sudden breathlessness.

'Have a business relationship.'

Oh, but Mark was so butter-smooth. *Stupid* of her to wait to hear from him the words he would never say.

Tiffany remembered the spark of malice in Brent's eyes—and tried to push it from her mind. 'You don't really think,' she said grimly, 'that Brent would switch stables just to make you angry?'

'You don't know the man.'

'I will,' she said.

The set of Mark's mouth was harder still. 'Sawyer is a notorious womaniser.'

'So you told me the first time I met him. I can look after myself.'

'Did he make advances to you?'

Tiffany hesitated.

'Did he?' Mark gripped her shoulders, his fingers biting into her skin. 'Brent Sawyer asked nothing of you except that you take in his horse?'

'Not really...'

Mark pounced on the words. 'Not really?' Earlier he had been the rugged outdoors man, familiar with horses, at home in the bush. Now he was the lawyer once more, relentless in his cross-examination of a reluctant witness, determined to unearth the facts.

'What did he want from you, Tiffany?'

'He asked me to have dinner with him.'

'Ah...'

'It isn't a crime, Mark. You've done a lot more than that. You've kissed me, caressed me—all against my will.'

'Never against your will,' he said harshly. 'Never once against your will. But to get back to Sawyer, I've warned you about his reputation. Did you accept his invitation?'

'I agreed to think about it.'

His fingers tightened. 'You will not go out with that man.'

Tiffany forced herself to ignore the rapid beating of her heart. All day she had yearned for Mark's touch, but this was not what she wanted from him, this angry, hostile, cruel grip.

'Do you think you can give me orders?' She flung the words at him furiously. 'Think again, if you think that. I will go out with anyone I please, Mark. *Anyone*.'

'Tiffany——'

'You may be the trustee of Andrew's money, and able to control my spending. But you do not control my social life. Not now, not ever.'

It had grown darker while they talked, so that it was impossible for Tiffany to see the tension lines in Mark's face, the pallor in his cheeks.

'I have to wonder,' he said at last, mockingly, 'what kind of a woman would be attracted to a man like Brent Sawyer?'

Tiffany wanted nothing more than to end the exchange. She felt a little ill at the thought that the lovely day was ending on such a bitter note. But she made herself reply coolly to Mark's question. 'A woman who is repulsed by strong-man antics. Brent may be a flirt, Mark, but he's also charming and very funny. I don't believe that he would ever lecture or threaten or pontificate.'

In the silence that followed her words, Tiffany heard the profanity that made it past Mark's lips. Abruptly, his hands fell to his hips.

'You dislike Brent so much,' she said slowly.

'He isn't to be trusted.'

'I asked you once if you saw us as two of a kind.'

'I will not get into this, Tiffany.'

But he had not bothered to deny the statement. Nothing would ever change, she thought painfully.

She lifted her head. 'I can't help it if you don't like Brent. I've agreed to stable his horse. I need every client I can get, and I will not go back on my agreement.'

'You don't have to see him socially.'

'Is that an order from my trustee?'

'It's a warning,' Mark said grimly.

CHAPTER NINE

FOR at least the third time that evening, Tiffany studied the list Mark had given her. Clarissa was on it, as well as three couples who were also called Donaldson. There were other names too, names like Langley and Minton and Plate, families in which the wives were relatives of Andrew's. After each name, in parenthesis, Mark had explained relationships with Andrew. He had also noted addresses and phone numbers.

On the table beside Tiffany was a stack of invitation cards which she had bought on her last trip into the city. She had debated with herself at some length whether to issue the invitations by post or by telephone, but in the end the post had won the day. Friendly and outgoing by nature, she was oddly reluctant to enter into impromptu conversations with people she did not know, and none of whom had thus far shown any sign of wanting to know her. Far better, she thought, to talk to Andrew's relatives face to face when she met them the first time.

Leaving her chair, she walked to the window where she stared thoughtfully out into the cricket-shrilling darkness. The sky was cloudless and studded with a myriad stars. Earlier in the day there had been some rain, unexpected and welcome, but of such short duration that it had done very little for the thirsty land. The only memory of the rain now was a freshness on the dusty air, and a few small puddles in places where the ground dipped a bit.

The barbecue... The enthusiasm with which Tiffany had put her idea to Mark in the restaurant had been replaced by a measure of uncertainty. Who were these people she was so eager to meet? How close were they to Clarissa?

And then there was Mark...

Several days had passed since their argument over Brent. It did not surprise Tiffany that she had not heard from Mark—she had not expected to. The question was, should she invite him to the barbecue? Would he come?

And did it matter?

Abruptly, she turned from the window. She would send out the invitations as planned. Mark must make up his own mind whether to accept. As must Clarissa. One way or another, she was going to have a party.

Sitting down at the table once more, she picked up the first card and began to write. She did not hesitate until she was almost at the end of the pack. Then she wrote Clarissa's name on one card, Mark's on the other.

The following morning, giving herself no time to change her mind, she drove to the nearest postbox and dropped the stamped envelopes through the slot.

The next days passed quickly. Tiffany's hours were so busy now that except at night, in the dreams that she could not seem to control, she had no time to brood about the man she loved.

Word of Donaldson's Place was spreading fast. Brent Sawyer arrived with his horse, which, not surprisingly, was a flashy-looking animal with the name Thunder. Every few days Brent would appear at the stables to go for a ride. Afterwards, he always hung around for a chat.

'Lovely lady,' he said, 'I gave you my office number once. I'm still waiting for you to phone me.'

'Mark Rowlands is my trustee, you know that, Brent.'

'You have a business here, sweet one—you may need someone to handle things for you. I'm talking about affairs that don't pertain to the trust.'

'But there is Mark...'

'The righteous Mark Rowlands.' Brent's eyes sparkled with familiar malice. 'The man who dots every "i", crosses every "t", who never bends even those rules which are meant to be broken. Aren't you bored with him? Don't tell me you've never thought of coming to me instead.'

It was one thing to be angry with Mark himself, another to hear him put down by someone else. 'Is this conversation ethical?' Tiffany asked carefully.

'Lovely lady, we're just having a friendly chat. Strictly off the record, you understand. There's no breach of ethics in that.'

Off the record... If ever Brent were censured for trying to seduce Tiffany away from Mark, he would deny the accusation, laugh it away as if it had never happened. Better acquainted with him now than she'd been at the start, Tiffany was able to understand Mark's hostility towards the other lawyer. She understood too that Mark's suspicions as well as her own had been well founded: Brent was a man who never did anything without a motive—his purpose in bringing his horse to Tiffany's stables had probably been to needle Mark.

But whatever his motives, Brent's manner was always as amusing as his comments were acerbic. It was rare for him to arrive without a few anecdotes, usually mischievous or a little off-colour, and though Tiffany saw him now for what he was, loneliness enabled her to tolerate his company. And Brent's presence did have a positive aspect—his money was helping to pay the bills, and he was bringing in other clients.

At every visit he asked the same question. 'Will you dine with me, gorgeous one?'

'No, thank you, Brent.'

'You break my heart, sweet lady,' he would say when she refused him, but so light-heartedly that it was obvious he did not expect her to take him seriously.

An advertisement in a small local paper had yielded response of another kind: several children and teenagers were now coming to the stables for riding lessons.

Fifteen-year-old Gillian Brewster was a natural horsewoman. She had always been able to ride, and now Tiffany was teaching her to jump. Watching the girl's prowess as the hurdles rose in height, Tiffany could only marvel at Gillian's potential.

An idea began to take shape in her mind. She mentioned it one afternoon, after Gillian had leaped exuberantly from Calypso's saddle.

'But that's *the* gymkhana of the year, Tiffany. Do you really think I can enter?'

'At this stage I'm just thinking about it—how would you feel about it, Gillian?'

The girl lifted a radiant face. 'It's my *dream* to be a show-jumper. It would be *wonderful* to win a trophy, but it wouldn't matter even if I didn't... Gosh, Tiffany, I can't wait to tell Mom and Dad about the gymkhana.'

Tiffany smiled at her. 'Steady on, I haven't quite made up my mind whether you should enter now or wait until next year.'

'Oh, but Tiffany...' The freckled young face was crestfallen.

'You want to be ready, Gillian. Besides, we still have lots of time to decide. Why don't we see how you get on in the next little while?'

Tiffany was still smiling as she watched Gillian mount her bicycle and ride away down the drive. Feisty and spirited, the fifteen-year-old was very much like Tiffany at the same age; perhaps that was why she felt such kinship with her. There was more than a chance that she would encourage Gillian to enter the gymkhana, but to tell her so too early would be to put too much pressure on the girl. Far better to let her improve her jumping a little more before making the competition a certainty.

And so Tiffany was very busy. Mornings were spent in the stables with the horses, afternoons giving riding lessons. In the early evening, she practised reading with Jonas.

There was a new teacher at the farm school, a woman with a keen interest in reading disabilities. Mrs Morrison was more than willing to give Jonas individual lessons, and when she heard that Tiffany was able to work with him at home as well, her enthusiasm increased. Jonas began to blossom as a result of so much focused attention. Even Betty now believed that her son would read.

It was only after dinner, when darkness fell upon the lonely farming country, that Tiffany had time to prepare for her party.

Wedged beneath a magnet on the fridge were evergrowing lists. Tiffany bought meat and fruit and salad ingredients, wine and nuts and chocolate. With Betty's help, she baked cakes and biscuits and stored them in her new freezer. On the afternoon before the party she sliced meat and onions and crisp green peppers into tiny cubes, and alternated them on pointed sticks: *shish kebabs*, ready for the flames.

'Refusals only' were the words printed at the bottom of the invitations, and Tiffany had received none of those—which boded well for the party. The only silence which puzzled her was Mark's. She did not know what to make of it; she tried not to think about it.

The phone rang on the evening before the party. Mark? Tiffany wondered, as she dusted some flour from her hands before picking up the receiver.

'This is Lucy Langley.' Andrew's third cousin had a deep and pleasant voice. 'I'm sorry, Miss Marlow, but I don't think my husband and I are going to be able to make it tomorrow.'

'What a pity!' Tiffany exclaimed. 'I was looking forward so much to meeting you both.'

'Yes, well...' Hesitation in the woman's voice. 'I really am sorry.'

'Can we arrange something else, Mrs Langley? Perhaps you'd like to come out to the house for lunch one day?'

'It's a little far out of town...'

'I drive into Bulawayo quite often; we could meet there.'

'I don't know...' The hesitation was more pronounced now: it came to Tiffany that Lucy Langley was sounding distinctly embarrassed. 'If you don't mind,' she said, 'let's just leave it alone for the moment.'

A little uneasily, Tiffany replaced the receiver. She was remembering a conversation with Clarissa, when that woman had been unwilling to meet her. But why was she thinking about that now? Clarissa's manner and Lucy Langley's could not have been more different.

Ten minutes later the phone rang once more. The caller was Belinda Donaldson, a distant niece of Andrew's by marriage. She was very sorry, she said, but she and her husband could not attend Tiffany's party. Like Lucy Langley, she was unwilling to make another arrangement.

By the time Anita Plate phoned, less than three minutes after that, Tiffany was no longer surprised.

'I'm wondering,' she said carefully, over the sick feeling in the pit of her stomach, 'why you waited until this evening to call me?'

'I don't think I understand...' The woman sounded as embarrassed as the previous callers.

'The invitations went out almost two weeks ago, Mrs Plate. When I didn't hear from you, I took it for granted that you were coming to my party.'

'Well, yes, that was our intention...'

'Did something happen?' It was a question Tiffany knew she had to ask.

'Not exactly...'

'What made you change your mind?'

'I'm sorry, Miss Marlow——' Anita Plate was sounding more and more upset '—it's a little hard for me to talk right now...'

Tiffany understood that there was no point in pressing her further. She heard a small sigh of relief as the woman said goodbye and put down the phone.

Other calls came after that. One after another, the invited guests phoned. All sounded hesitant, troubled, embarrassed and upset. No explanations were given as to why the refusals were so late in coming, no offers were made to meet at another time.

One by one, Tiffany grimly crossed the names from her list. Eventually, only two names remained—Clarissa and Mark.

Clarissa phoned very late that evening.

'Miss Marlow? So sorry, but I won't be coming tomorrow. Your lovely party, I was so looking forward to it. *Such* a pity, I'm really awfully sorry.'

In contrast to the callers who had preceded her, Clarissa sounded bright, animated and gushy. Not one bit sorry. Tiffany's hand tightened on the receiver. There were things she would have liked to tell Clarissa Donaldson, but she resisted the temptation. Voice as cold as she could make it, she said, 'I was expecting you to phone,' and firmly put down the receiver.

One more call to go. But by midnight Mark had not phoned.

Next morning, Tiffany looked at the lists she had made. She looked at the *shish kebabs* in the fridge, the cakes which were still in the freezer. Betty, who normally sang while she worked around the house, was silent, her pleasant face mortified. Jonas was subdued too. Tiffany was beyond being mortified, she was filled with a terrible rage.

By midday, Mark still had not phoned. Ignoring Betty's pleas not to go out alone, Tiffany decided to go for a run. Before long she had left the boundary of her own property far behind her. She ran down country roads which, until now, she had seen only through the car windscreen. She ran across a stretch of *veld* where burrs and blackjacks attached themselves to her jeans. She paused once to watch a troop of monkeys swinging in the trees, paused again when she tripped over loose stones and fell to the ground winded.

She had forgotten how hot it was until she lay on the prickly scrub and struggled to catch her breath. She was panting, her clothes were moist with sweat. Picking herself up, she began to make her way back.

In the kitchen, a concerned Betty was waiting with a long glass of iced tea.

Tiffany gave the housekeeper a grateful smile. 'You are so good to me.'

'You are good to us, Tiffany. Jonas and I don't like to see you upset.'

'I guess there are worse things in life than being stood up. Anyone phone while I was out?'

'No.' Betty was unable to meet her eyes.

Damn Mark Rowlands! Damn the man! At least Andrew's relatives had had the grace, dubious though it was, to tell her that they were not coming. Mark was letting her down without even that much consideration.

The day wore on. Tiffany filled the hours with all the chores she could think of. By late afternoon there had still been no word from Mark.

She had to get out of the house again. This time she saddled Calypso and galloped away through the *veld*. The horse, so gentle with children, seemed to understand her mood, her need for speed. Responsive to her slightest command, Calypso jumped low fences and dried-out streams, galloped through grassy areas, dodged trees and rocks. And finally, when Tiffany's restlessness had eased, the horse slowed its gait to a walk.

By the time Tiffany turned Calypso in the direction of home, it was darker than she had realised. As she neared the barn, she saw someone leaning against the wall.

'Jonas,' she called, 'I'm sorry if I...'

The words stopped in her throat as the person straightened. He was much taller than Jonas, not a boy but a man.

'*Mark*?' The name emerged hoarsely from Tiffany's throat as he came towards her.

'Hello, Tiffany.'

He was looking up at her, his eyes narrowed, the expression in the rugged face hard to read.

She was about to turn the horse, to gallop away once more, when Mark's hand went to Calypso's bridle.

'Get down,' he ordered quietly.

'No...'

'Now.' His tone was authoritative, brooking no argument.

Tiffany sat in the saddle, glaring down at him.

'What are you doing here?' she demanded.

An autocratic eyebrow lifted. 'You invited me to a party.'

'No one is coming.'

'I'm here.'

Tiffany searched Mark's face. A hint of pity, and she would ride away from him. But there was no pity in his expression.

Blinking back tears, she lifted her chin. 'Stood up at the eleventh hour.'

'Get down from that horse, Tiffany.'

'I don't think you understand...'

The hand on the bridle lifted, and now he was holding out both hands to her. 'I understand, rose nymph.'

She looked at him wordlessly. And then she was dismounting, and Mark's hands were on her waist as her feet touched the ground. Riding off into the bush earlier, Tiffany had been angry enough to take on the whole world. As Mark's arm went around her shoulders, the fight went out of her.

Jonas was nowhere to be seen. Only later would Tiffany learn that Mark had told the boy that he would take care of the horse himself.

Mark's arm was still around her shoulders as they walked into the barn. He nudged Tiffany aside when she would have seen to Calypso. Protest rose to her lips, and died. Mutely, she leaned back against the wall, inhaling the familiar odours of horse and hay, the odours of the one world that was entirely her own, and watched Mark do the things that Jonas normally did, and which Mark seemed to do just as well.

When Calypso was settled, Mark turned to her. 'Come, Tiffany.'

'Why did they do it?' She lifted her head and looked at him. 'Mark, why?'

'Sweetheart . . .'

The endearment was Tiffany's undoing. To her horror, she began to cry. She had kept her head high all day, the run and the ride through the windswept *veld* the only antidote to her frustrations. But there was no stopping the tears now. She cried as if her heart would break.

In an instant, Mark had closed the gap between them. His arms went around Tiffany, holding her close to him as she wept.

'Why?' she asked when she could speak again.

She felt his lips move in her hair, and her heart did a strange little somersault in her chest. Oh, but she had missed being close to him.

'They shouldn't have done it to you,' he said against her ear.

'If they were going to refuse, they could have done so right away—but there wasn't a peep out of even one of them, not until last night. I was so certain they were coming, Mark. All my plans were made, Betty and I baked and cooked.' She lifted her head from his chest.

'Why did they wait so long to phone? *How could they be so cruel*?'

'Perhaps they didn't mean to be,' Mark said, his voice sounding so odd.

Tiffany was suddenly outraged. 'How can you say that?' she demanded. 'They all knew what they were doing, they must have known.' She paused, remembering the sequence of telephone calls. 'It was the strangest thing, Mark, one call after another. All those people, speaking almost the same words. As if they were in a play, as if they were acting on cue.'

Mark was silent. Tiffany stood quietly in the circle of his arms, his maleness in her nostrils, the beating of his heart and the roughness of his sweater against her throat. She forced herself to ignore the desire stirring within her—the sensory part of her craving the joy of Mark's lovemaking, the rational part knowing there were things she had to think about instead.

'On cue...' she said thoughtfully. 'The timing of the calls couldn't have been coincidence... That's it, Mark! They *were* all acting on cue.'

Still Mark did not answer, but he was so close to her that she felt the sudden bunching of his muscles.

All at once, Tiffany understood. '*Clarissa*!' she exclaimed, throwing back her head. 'She told them not to come. *Ordered* them not to. She did, didn't she, Mark? I know I'm right! Hers was the last call of the lot. She pretended to be sorry, but it was obvious that she wasn't. It's not news that Clarissa doesn't like me, but what about the rest of them?'

'Think about it,' Mark said.

'Andrew's will,' Tiffany responded slowly.

'I tried to warn you.'

'I remember... Was I very naïve to think they'd come to terms with it? I'm still the outsider, still the manipulator. That's it, isn't it?'

Mark was silent. His arms tightened around her.

Tiffany jerked away from him. 'Couldn't they have given me a chance? I invited them to a party. I wanted to meet them, have them meet me. We could have talked, could have got to know each other.' She pushed a hand through her tousled windswept hair. 'Now that I think of it, perhaps they did want to come. They were so apologetic, Mark. Except for Clarissa, they all sounded embarrassed.'

'They're not bad people, Tiffany.'

'And yet they follow Clarissa's orders. She dictates, and the clan listens. Why, Mark? Will you tell me?'

'You have to understand Clarissa's position,' he said slowly. 'Her father was a rich and powerful man. There are Donaldson interests which he controlled, which Clarissa now controls in his place.'

'Giving her a hold over the whole family? She waves her demon stick, and they do her bidding like lambs?' Tiffany pressed her hands to her temples, where two hammers of pain were beginning to pound. 'I've tried so hard, but there's more here than I can fight.'

'Fight, Tiffany?'

'If it were just Clarissa, I think I could deal with that. But you've both been against me from the start.'

Mark cupped her face in his hands. 'I've never wanted to think badly of you, Tiffany.'

Something in his tone made the blood race in her veins. 'And yet you do.'

'There are facts that have been difficult to ignore.'

'Facts which you misunderstood.'

'I want very much to believe you, Tiffany.'

'When will you, Mark?'

They were still in the barn. There were lights now which had not been there previously, but where Tiffany and Mark stood, in the shadows, it was quite dark. Earlier, when she was weeping, Tiffany had welcomed the darkness: now, as she strained her eyes to look at

Mark, she wished that she could make out his expression more clearly.

'Perhaps I'm beginning to,' he said.

'*Mark*...' The name emerged on a wild surge of hope.

'Give it time, Tiffany,' he said.

He drew her to him again. He began to kiss her, so passionately that small sounds of pleasure emerged from her throat. His tongue pushed into her mouth, exploring its sweetness, and she welcomed him there. She wanted him inside her, all of him... And it did not matter that she had sent him away when he'd tried to make love to her. If he wanted to take her to bed now, she would not be able to stop him. Forgotten was the barbecue, forgotten the guests and their brutal rejection. Now Mark was the only reality.

But after a long while, he lifted his head. 'I came here for a party.'

'A party...' She was dazed. It was an effort to think.

'What about it, Tiffany?'

'A party for two?' she asked unsteadily.

He laughed softly. 'A party for two is sometimes the best.'

Her head was beginning to clear. 'There's so much food. What on earth will I do with it all?'

He touched her cheek in the way she remembered and loved. 'You and I will eat a bit. Betty and Jonas will enjoy some too. You can freeze the rest.'

'You're a practical man, Mark Rowlands.'

He traced his thumb around her lips. 'Do we have a party, rose nymph?'

Tiffany was glad it was dark, for she knew that her heart was in her eyes as she smiled at him. 'Yes, we do.'

And so the evening was rescued in a way that Tiffany could not have imagined earlier.

Long after they had eaten, they sat on the veranda with a bottle of wine, and talked. They had so much catching up to do. Mark told Tiffany a little more about the case he'd been working on. She told him how the stables were progressing. Purposely, she omitted any mention of Brent, talking instead about the children she was teaching. In particular, she told him about Gillian Brewster.

'She was so excited when I finally gave her the go-ahead to enter the gymkhana. She dreams of becoming a show-jumper. I wish you could see her, Mark—she's so talented.'

'I'll see her,' he said.

Tiffany sat forward in her chair. 'You'll be at the gymkhana?'

'Yes, I will.' On a different note, he added, 'Someone else will be there too.'

'Clarissa,' Tiffany said dully. 'I remember now, you told me that she has some involvement with show-jumping. Is she a jumper too?'

'She used to be. You have to know, Tiffany, Clarissa traditionally hosts a reception after the event.'

Tiffany's hands tightened in her lap. 'So what if she does? It's nothing to do with me.'

'The riders and their parents are always invited. The teachers too.'

'Not this teacher.'

'It may look strange if you don't attend.'

'To whom, Mark? To Clarissa? She boycotted my party; she won't expect me at hers.'

'Gillian may want to go.'

'It's up to her to go if she wants.'

'I will be at the party, Tiffany.'

Tiffany's nails dug into the soft palms of her hands, and she swallowed down hard on the vile taste in her throat. Strange how she kept forgetting that Mark had had a life before her arrival in Zimbabwe. A life that had included Clarissa, still included her evidently.

Minutes ago there had been magic in the evening. Now there was only tension.

'I don't see myself going to a party of Clarissa's,' she said.

'Think about it, Tiffany.'

But Tiffany shook her head. 'There's absolutely nothing to think about.'

CHAPTER TEN

GILLIAN was improving every day. Horse and rider were a joy to watch. Sleekly, swiftly they rode around the paddock, the horse jumping the hurdles with a fluid grace, the rider poised and fearless on its back. Each day, as the bars went up another notch, the pair rose to the challenge and gave even more of themselves to the effort.

Tiffany leaned her elbows on the wooden paddock fence, smiling as she watched them. From the moment she had entered Gillian in the gymkhana, the girl's eagerness and enthusiasm had known no limits. Had Tiffany allowed her to do so, she would willingly have spent every waking hour practising in the paddock. As it was, Tiffany thought sometimes that Gillian spent almost too much time on her horse.

She was about to call out to her, to tell her it was time to end her practice, when a long shadow fell suddenly across the sun-baked ground.

'This is a surprise,' Tiffany said gladly. 'I wasn't expecting you here today, Mark.'

'Hello, Tiffany.'

There was a curtness in his voice, but in her joy at seeing him, Tiffany made nothing of it.

He gestured. 'Gillian?'

'Yes. Isn't she fantastic? Watch her take that next jump. There... *Oh, good girl, Gillian*! I try to see her with the eyes of a judge, but I'm not sure if I'm too prejudiced.'

'She's good,' Mark said.

This time Tiffany registered his brusqueness. Taken aback, she turned her attention from the paddock to the man she loved.

What she saw in his face chilled her. There was an ominous cynicism in his eyes, a hardness in his lips, an autocratic tilt to his head, none of which spoke for a relaxed visit.

'Is something wrong?' she asked uncertainly.

His eyes moved towards the girl on the horse. 'Lesson nearly over?'

'Just about. What is it, Mark?'

'We'll talk when she's gone.'

'You have me worried.'

Mark would touch her cheek now in the gesture she loved so much, and assure her that she was imagining things. But he did nothing of the kind. If anything, the cynicism in his eyes increased, and his lips tightened in an inflexible line.

Frightened suddenly, Tiffany put her hand on his arm. 'Talk to me, Mark!'

In an instant, the muscles beneath her fingers grew rigid. Abruptly Mark removed his arm from her hand and turned his head towards the paddock. Tiffany saw the stiffness in his back and neck, and her heart began to thud uncomfortably in her chest.

'How was that, Tiffany?' Gillian called out.

Tiffany forced herself to concentrate on the girl. No matter how worried she was, Gillian was working hard and deserved her attention.

'Excellent,' she called back. 'Your best round ever.'

'Shall I try again?'

A quick glance at her watch. 'No more today. You've been at it long enough; you don't want to tire the horse.'

Gillian rode once more around the paddock, then vaulted neatly to the ground. Holding the reins, she came to the fence. 'Hello,' she said shyly to Mark. And to

Tiffany, 'I can't believe the gymkhana is just over a week away. Same time tomorrow?'

'Same time tomorrow,' Tiffany managed to say steadily.

Gillian led the horse to the barn, where Jonas was waiting for her. She must have helped him wipe the horse down, for it was some minutes before she reappeared. With a cheerful goodbye to Tiffany, a more subdued one to Mark, she threw her leg over her bicycle and rode away.

When Gillian had vanished from sight, Tiffany drew a calming breath and turned to Mark.

'Talk to me,' she said.

His eyes raked her face in a look that was anything but lover-like. The eyes of a predator, waiting to pounce on its helpless prey, Tiffany thought, and shuddered.

'Don't keep me in suspense,' she said over a throat that was suddenly so dry that it was difficult to swallow.

'Expecting any more students?' he asked abruptly.

'Gillian was the last one today. Do... do you want to go up to the house? We can sit on the veranda.'

'No.'

'It's shadier there. I can get us something cool to drink...'

'Nothing to drink,' he said roughly.

'What is it, Mark?' She was really frightened now. 'Why are you here?'

'To get the truth from you, finally.'

She lifted her head at his insolence. 'I've never told you anything but the truth.'

'Is that so?' he asked mockingly. Thrusting his hand deep into the pocket of his trousers, he pulled out an envelope. 'You have some explaining to do. And only the truth will do this time, Tiffany.'

She watched him take a folded sheet of paper from the envelope. Without knowing quite why, she began to tremble.

'What is that?'

'Don't you know?'

'Should I?'

'Damn right you should.'

'Some mistake at the bank?' She ventured a tiny smile. 'What is it, Mark? I may have done something silly, but whatever it is, it can hardly be a crime.'

'That's exactly what it is.' His tone was heavy with distaste.

'*What on earth are you talking about*?'

'This!' Savagely, Mark thrust the paper at Tiffany. 'And if you're thinking of destroying it, save yourself the bother—I have a photocopy.'

With trembling fingers, Tiffany took the paper from his hand. It was covered with writing. Her own writing; she recognised it immediately. It took a few seconds longer for her to read the first few lines.

Tension had created a hard knot of pain in her stomach, but somehow she managed to draw herself up straight. 'Well?'

'You're not going to pretend you didn't write this?'

'No, of course not. Why would I?'

'It's incriminating to say the least.'

Over the dryness in her throat, she said, 'Is it?' Her eyes returned to the paper. 'How did you get this anyway?'

'In the mail,' he told her grimly. 'That surprises you, doesn't it, Tiffany? One nasty bit of evidence you never expected to turn up.'

'Evidence!' she repeated angrily. 'You make me sound like a felon.'

'Felon? An apt word indeed. That innocent face of yours, Tiffany. The sweetness. As a lawyer, my instincts told me to be careful of you. As a man I found myself succumbing to your loveliness. I wanted so much to believe you, it isn't long since I told you that. How you must have laughed at me, Tiffany.'

'No,' she said through trembling lips.

'It must have amused you to see me falling for you.'

She felt desperate. 'That isn't true.'

'So alluring, Tiffany, so very seductive. And so devious.'

'*Stop it*!' Tiffany covered her ears in an attempt to shut out the terrible things Mark was saying.

But he pulled her hands down. 'You were beginning to fool me, just as you fooled poor Andrew.'

'You don't know what you're saying!'

'Don't I, Tiffany?'

'Nothing has changed.' She was shaking quite violently now. 'There's no reason for you to turn on me like this.'

'Everything has changed,' he retorted savagely.

Feeling more ill by the moment, Tiffany stared at him. 'You haven't answered my question.'

'Which question was that?'

'How you came by this.'

'It was sent to me by Andrew's British lawyer. That surprises you, doesn't it? I'd asked Barnett for certain documents, and somehow this bit of paper must have slipped in at the same time. I don't think he intended me to have it.'

'But you read it anyway.'

'Of course.'

'And drew your conclusions.'

'They weren't hard to draw, Tiffany. You always denied persuading Andrew to make you his beneficiary.'

'I still do.'

'You're really quite brazen, aren't you?' The disgust in Mark's expression was so intense now that Tiffany found she could not look at him. He jerked his head towards the paper in her hand. 'What's written there amounts to a lot more than a bit of persuasion. You wrote out these instructions yourself and sent them to Andrew's lawyer.'

'Mark...'

His eyes were hard with loathing. 'Do you deny it?'

'No...'

'In other words, you admit that you told Barnett exactly how to draw Andrew's will.'

'It's not the way you think it is, Mark.'

'I'll be the judge of that,' he said coldly. 'Tell me this, did Andrew have any idea that you were instructing his lawyer to draw his will in your favour?'

'Of course he did.'

'More lies, Tiffany?'

'They're not lies, Mark. The things that are written here were Andrew's wishes.'

'Why go on with this, Tiffany? You're only making things worse for yourself.'

'You have to believe me! These...these instructions really were Andrew's wishes. I didn't want to be his beneficiary. I tried to persuade him to leave his estate to his relatives. He wouldn't hear of it.'

'Why not?'

'We've been over this a hundred times.'

'Let's go over it again.'

For the first time in her life Tiffany had a sense of what it must be like to be trapped in a witness box by a hostile lawyer. To tell the truth, and have every word dismissed as a lie.

'Andrew had lost all contact with his relatives, he said they meant nothing to him. While I...' She stopped helplessly.

Mark finished the sentence for her. 'While you were in his house. So young and lovely. So seemingly innocent. And so damnably seductive. Oh, yes, Tiffany, I can see it all. I know exactly what happened.'

'No,' she said desperately, 'you don't know. Andrew refused to listen to my arguments. He insisted that he wanted me to be his beneficiary.'

'You make him sound like a strong man, a man with a will of his own.'

'He was that.'

'Why didn't he instruct his lawyer himself, in that case?'

At no other time had Tiffany been quite so desperate to tell Mark the truth. She opened her mouth to speak, the words trembled on her tongue, but she choked them back. She had given Andrew a promise; she could not break it.

'Why didn't Andrew write out the instructions himself, Tiffany?'

'He asked me to do it for him,' she said faintly. 'Isn't that enough for you?'

'No. I asked you this once before, Tiffany—was there a reason why Andrew couldn't have attended to his own affairs?'

Tiffany put a hand to a head that felt as if it would burst with pain. 'No.'

'Was he mentally competent?'

She met his eyes. 'As competent as you and I.'

'I see.'

'No, you don't, and I can't explain it to you. Mark, please...'

Impulsively she touched his hand, but, as if the contact repulsed him, Mark jerked his hand away. Tiffany felt the blood drain from her cheeks. Her legs were so weak all at once that she had to clutch the paddock fence for support.

'How can I make you believe me?'

'I don't think you can. I look at you, Tiffany, and I'm filled with disgust. You took advantage of a defenceless man, you deprived his relatives of what should have been theirs. You...' He stopped.

'What?' she whispered.

Mark had never looked more dangerous, more forbidding. 'You realised I was attracted to you, and you played on my emotions. You knew I was coming very close to...' Once more, he stopped.

Tiffany held her breath, waiting for him to finish the sentence.

'It doesn't matter,' he said harshly. 'It's over now anyway.'

Turning abruptly, he began to walk away from her.

'Mark...' she called. And when he turned, 'What happens now?'

The dark eyes were bleak. 'I don't know.'

'Are you still my trustee?'

'I can't tell you.'

'Are you thinking of fighting Andrew's bequest?'

'I'll be doing some serious thinking.'

Tiffany was shaking. 'You won't... You can't try to close down my stables?'

'I don't know what I'll do.' Mark's voice was like ice. 'I'll let you know when I've made some decisions.'

It was with a heavy heart that Tiffany entered the gymkhana grounds with Gillian. The girl had decided to travel to the event with Tiffany rather than with her parents, who would be joining them later. They had arranged separate transport for Firefly, Gillian's horse.

Looking pretty and trim in new jodhpurs, boots and hat, Gillian did not stop talking for a second. Though Tiffany was finding it difficult to respond lightly to the constant chatter, she made a valiant effort. She could not let her own low spirits affect the girl who had worked so hard to prepare herself for her first competitive event.

'I'm scared,' Gillian said suddenly.

Tiffany gave her a reassuring smile. 'That's understandable.'

'I can't go through with it!'

'Of course you can. It's natural to feel nervous, just remember that you're a really fine jumper.'

'I feel sick, Tiffany. I do. Oh, God, I think I should go home.'

Tiffany had experienced stage-fright with other young jumpers. Putting her arm around the girl's shoulders, she gave her a warm hug. 'Run along, Gillian. It's time to join the other competitors.'

'I can't! Oh, God, Tiffany...' Gillian wailed.

'I'll be holding thumbs for you.'

'I'll disgrace you, I know I will.'

'And I know that you'll make me very proud. Go now, Gillian.'

The girl hesitated a moment longer. Then she pushed at her new hat, made a comical face, and walked away.

Tiffany felt a sense of isolation as she began to make her way towards her seat. The world of horses, of riding and jumping, was relatively small: acquaintances stood everywhere in sociable groups. In England, Tiffany would also have met people she knew; in Zimbabwe she was the outsider.

She paused when she saw a face she recognised. Brent had not seen her. For a moment Tiffany thought of joining him. But the moment passed, and she walked on. Lonely or not, there was only one man she wanted to be with. It made no sense that even now, when that man despised her, no substitute would do.

Where are you, Mark? she wondered as she waited in her seat for the gymkhana to begin. Two weeks had gone by since their last disastrous meeting. Two weeks of uncertainty, for who knew what Mark, with his worst suspicions about her confirmed, would now do? She remembered telling him once that if he did not let her have access to her money she would approach a bank for a loan. Theoretically, he could not close down her stables; practically speaking, it was difficult to know how sympathetic a bank would be to her situation. If Mark took a hard line, he might just make it impossible for her to carry on.

Tiffany's spirits lifted only when the jumping began. This was her world, and she knew and loved every part of it: the grace of the riders, the agility of the horses, the pleasure of seeing hurdles cleared, the tension when a horse balked or a bar came down, the elation when a round was well performed. When there was good rapport between a horse and its rider, the jumps looked so effortless. Only the rider and the coach knew the full extent of the work that went into preparing for such an event.

And then it was Gillian's turn. Saying a silent prayer, Tiffany sat tensely at the edge of her seat.

Spectators watching the girl as she rode confidently into the arena could not have guessed at her earlier nervousness. When she took Firefly skilfully over the first hurdles, they would not have known that she had not been jumping long.

'*Yes*!' Tiffany shouted exultantly as horse and rider cleared one of the more difficult hurdles. '*Yes*, *Gillian*, *yes*!' The girl was riding beautifully, faultlessly, remembering every instruction Tiffany had ever given her.

Horse and rider were almost at the end of the track when Firefly's hind hooves caught a bar and sent it flying to the ground. The hurdle had given other riders problems as well. Tiffany drew in her breath, but to her relief Gillian recovered herself well. With all the poise of a seasoned show-jumper, she rode further, cleared two more hurdles, and completed the round. She was smiling as she left the arena to enthusiastic applause.

Satisfied, Tiffany sat back in her seat. Not a perfect score, but oh, Gillian had done well.

The awards ceremony came soon after that. Tiffany was delighted when Gillian received the award for the most promising young rider.

She had left the stands when a hand touched her arm. Turning, she found herself face to face with Gillian's parents.

'An award was the last thing we expected.' Arlene Brewster's eyes shone.

Tiffany smiled at them both. 'Gillian deserved it. Wasn't she fantastic?'

'She certainly did us proud. As her teacher, you should have been up there too, collecting a prize,' Simon Brewster said.

'Thanks, but I don't think I can take that much credit. You should have seen Gillian practising hour after hour in the paddock. She deserves that award.'

'You're too modest, Tiffany,' Gillian's father said. 'Arlene and I know how much you did for our daughter. You'll have students beating a path to your door after this, we'll make sure of that.'

Tiffany decided not to tell these very nice people that if her unforgiving trustee had his way the doors of her stables could well be in danger of closing.

'Thank you,' was all she said.

They were still talking when Gillian came bounding up. A radiant Gillian, her smile wide, her eyes sparkling.

Her parents kissed her, and Tiffany gave her a hug.

'It was so exciting!' Gillian said, when they had all congratulated her. 'I enjoyed every moment—can you believe it? I mean, after being so nervous, after wanting to give the whole thing a skip? Even knocking down the bar didn't upset me too much.' The words tumbled from her lips. 'By the way,' she went on, 'we're all invited to Clarissa Donaldson's party. We can go, can't we?'

Arlene Brewster looked impressed. 'I've read about Clarissa Donaldson—she's an important figure in the show-jumping world. Are you related to her, Tiffany?'

'The stables are named after the previous owner of the property.' Tiffany's lips felt stiff. 'Look, about the party... I... I won't be going to it.'

'Tiffany, you must!' Gillian insisted.

'I don't think so...'

'I'm dying to go!' With the urgency of her ride over, Gillian was once again an impetuous fifteen-year-old.

Tiffany forced a smile. 'You'll go with your parents, Gillian. I'm not really one for big parties.'

Simon Brewster stepped forward. 'It would mean a lot to us all if you came.'

Another refusal hovered on Tiffany's tongue, but she closed her lips when she saw Gillian's face. Some of the excitement had left the girl's eyes, and she was watching Tiffany anxiously. It came to Tiffany that Gillian would be very disappointed if she did not go to the party. And she knew that on this one day it would be selfish if she insisted on putting her own feelings first.

'Please come,' Gillian pleaded.

There would be so many people at the party: jumpers, parents, teachers. People associated with the world of horses and riders. Tiffany would not be expected to spend any time socialising with Clarissa. A few conventionally formal words to that lady would be sufficient.

'All right,' she said slowly.

'Wow!' Gillian threw her arms around Tiffany and gave her a hug. 'Oh, this is going to be great! Let's go!'

There were a few things Tiffany needed to do before she left the grounds, and so it was arranged that Gillian would go ahead with her parents.

Minutes after she had said goodbye to the Brewsters, Tiffany turned a corner and came face to face with Mark and Clarissa. For one tense second she wondered whether they would stop. Mark, she thought, might have walked on, but Clarissa stood still in front of her.

'Why, Tiffany, I was just commenting to Mark that we hadn't seen you around.' Clarissa put a hand on Mark's arm. 'Isn't that right, darling?'

On Mark's bare skin, the hand with its long scarlet-painted nails had a predatory look. Tiffany suppressed a shudder.

'Darling?' Clarissa repeated.

'Right.' Mark's tone was abrupt.

He was making no effort to dislodge the possessive hand. Nor, Tiffany noted unhappily, did he look any more affable than at their last meeting. His expression was impersonal, his eyes bleak.

'Splendid jumper, your little protégée. Have to watch her, she'll be walking off with all the major prizes before long,' Clarissa prattled on happily. As if, Tiffany thought grimly, she were some artless *ingénue*, as if she had not deliberately set out to ruin Tiffany's barbecue.

'She's a good jumper,' she agreed shortly.

'I invited her to my party. Of course, as her teacher, you are invited too.'

'Gillian did convey the invitation, thank you.'

'You will be coming, won't you?' A brilliant smile.

Still that artless voice. But behind the smile, a shrewd watchfulness lurked.

Tiffany glanced once more at Mark. If anything, his expression had grown even more forbidding than before. The manicured hand still clung to his bare arm. Tiffany wished the sight of it didn't hurt her so much. He doesn't want me to come to the party, she thought. Neither of them wants me there. All the more reason to attend. Very often the fighting spirit came to Tiffany when she needed it most; it came to her now.

Her head lifted proudly. 'Thank you, Clarissa, I wouldn't miss it,' she said, and had the satisfaction of seeing the brilliant smile falter momentarily in the beautiful face.

Mark and Clarissa walked on together. Tiffany watched them numbly. Now that her brief moment of outrage had passed, she wondered how on earth she would get through the party. She would be alone, Clarissa would be with Mark.

A thought came, and she looked hurriedly around her. People had begun to leave the grounds—she might be too late. And then she saw him, a little distance away, walking in the direction of the car park.

'Brent!' she called, running to catch up with him.

He turned, and smiled. 'If it isn't the teacher whose name will be on all lips after today. I looked for you everywhere.'

'I've been invited to Clarissa Donaldson's party. Will you come with me, Brent?'

He looked intrigued. 'I won't be Clarissa's most favoured guest.'

'Do you care?'

'Not in the least.' His eyes were alight with the familiar spark of malice. 'I would be delighted to come with you, fairest lady. My limo awaits you.'

'Thanks, but I do have my car here. I'll meet you at the Donaldson house, Brent.'

The party was in full swing by the time they arrived. Tiffany tried not to feel too awed as she walked into Clarissa's house. It was very large and immensely ornate. Guests thronged the spacious front rooms: like Tiffany, many of them were still dressed in the jodhpurs they had worn to the gymkhana.

Gillian ran up, delighted that Tiffany had arrived, but after a minute or two she left to chatter excitedly to a friend. The Brewsters were nowhere to be seen. Looking around rooms crowded with people she had never met, Tiffany was very glad that she had thought of inviting an escort.

'Impressed by the grandeur?' Brent asked with an irreverent grin.

'Overwhelmed,' she responded drily.

Brent laughed. 'You are delicious.'

A moment later, without any warning, he bent his head and kissed a startled Tiffany full on the lips.

The kiss did not last more than a few seconds. As Brent straightened, Tiffany took a startled step backwards. She felt someone watching her. Instinctively turning her head, she caught Mark staring at her in disgust across the room. Their eyes held for a long moment. Mark turned away then, and Tiffany began to talk animatedly, and inanely, to Brent.

The heat in the house was so intense that Tiffany's head began to throb. It was becoming more and more difficult to keep up a conversation with Brent. Mark was always on the periphery of her vision, Clarissa never far from his side.

Tiffany was glad when Brent suggested a walk in the garden. Floodlights lit the lawn and sparkled over a kidney-shaped pool. The evening air was pleasant, the sound of lapping water relaxing. Tiffany's headache began to fade, but her throat was uncomfortably dry. When Brent offered to fetch them some drinks, she accepted gratefully.

Left alone, she knelt down beside the pool and let her fingers trail in the warm water. When footsteps sounded behind her, she said in surprise, 'Brent, you were quick.'

He did not speak, but she sensed him towering above her. Curiously, she lifted her head. In a moment the breath caught in her throat.

'*Mark*!'

'You look happy to see me,' he mocked.

'You must have followed us outside,' she accused.

'How astute of you.'

'And waited until Brent went to get us some drinks.'

'Right, again.'

Her heartbeat quickened. 'Why would you do that?'

'I'll ask the questions,' Mark said, and she heard the danger in his voice. 'What is Brent Sawyer doing here?'

'He came with me,' Tiffany responded evenly.

'He wasn't invited.'

'Did you see the mob in that house? One more person can't make much difference. Besides, I assumed I was entitled to an escort.'

'You were,' Mark said impatiently. 'My question is, why Sawyer?'

'He's as pleasant as anyone else.'

'Don't give me that, Tiffany. You know how I feel about the man—is that why you invited him?'

Tiffany's head was beginning to ache once more, but she forced herself to maintain an outer calm. 'Really, Mark, you flatter yourself if you think that I would go to so much effort just to thwart you. Don't you understand that your feelings are a matter of complete indifference to me?'

'You little bitch,' he said roughly, seizing her hands and tugging her to her feet.

'Let me go!' she shouted.

'When I'm ready to,' Mark taunted. 'It's a long time since I kissed you, Tiffany. Have you been missing it? Is that why you were so eager to let that swine Sawyer kiss you in public?'

'Actually, I enjoyed it.' She took pleasure in the lie, in hearing the furious hiss of his breath.

'That was not my impression,' he said contemptuously. 'But you will enjoy this, I promise you.'

She tried to pull away from him. 'I'll hate it!' she shouted. 'I'm warning you, Mark, don't try it!'

She meant what she said. She had missed Mark every day of the last two weeks, yet she could not let him kiss her out of provocation or revenge.

But Mark ignored her protests. Laughing into her face, he began to draw her against him. Fury at that laughter gave Tiffany strength. Pushing hard at his chest, she wrenched herself free of him.

They were closer to the edge of the pool than either of them had realised. Mark took a step backwards—and fell into the water. Tiffany was appalled, but only for a moment; then she burst out laughing. Oh, but it was lovely to see Mark Rowlands humbled!

Her amusement did not last long, only as long as it took Mark to surface. With a quick snake-like movement, he reached for one of her ankles and pulled her in with him.

Tiffany tried to get away from him, but Mark's arms went around her before she could pull herself out of the pool. She saw his head come down and tried to escape him, but he was stronger than she was, and after a few moments she lost the will to resist.

His kisses were relentless, possessive, his tongue forcing its way between her lips as his arms welded her body to his. A familiar dizzying excitement surged through Tiffany's veins, heating her blood, quickening her senses. The water swirled around them as she lifted her arms around Mark's neck and began to respond to his kisses. He was pulling her against him, closer and closer, chest against chest, stomach against stomach, hips and thighs welded together. Tiffany's feet did not touch the ground, but when she flailed, Mark clamped her ankles firmly between his legs. Their wet clothes clung to them like skin—it was as if they were both naked. His maleness throbbed against her, hard and powerful, and so erotic that Tiffany forgot that this man was her enemy, had always been her enemy, that he distrusted her, that he had pulled her into the pool only as punishment.

They kissed passionately, frenziedly, as if they could not get enough of each other, as if the time apart had created a thirst that could not be slaked. Mark pulled at her shirt, and then his tongue was a hard stroke down her throat and over her breasts, and his teeth were at her hardened nipples, and she was arching back her head exultantly, so that he could get closer still...

And then someone yelled, 'What the hell is going on here?'

A second later Brent had jumped into the pool. An uncharacteristically angry Brent. Mark released Tiffany with a muttered oath. Tiffany screamed as Brent landed a punch to Mark's face.

The two men were exchanging punches, the water heaving feverishly around them, as Tiffany pulled herself out of the pool. She did not stay to see the outcome of the fight. Water was dripping from her clothes as she ran to her car.

An hour later Tiffany stopped in front of her house. So weary was she that it was too much of an effort to open the door and get out of the car. Her hair was matted, her clothes sticky and uncomfortable. Shivering a little, she leaned back against the damp seat. And then she put her hands over her eyes and began to weep.

CHAPTER ELEVEN

'THAT was very good, Jonas. Excellent, in fact.'

'Really, Tiffany?'

Tiffany smiled at the bright-eyed boy sitting next to her at the kitchen table. 'I wouldn't say it if I didn't mean it.'

Jonas had come a long way since the day when he had fled the yard in shame because he could not read the instructions on a tin of varnish. As it had turned out, his learning difficulties had not been quite as severe as either his mother or Tiffany had feared, and by now much of his problem had been remedied. Whatever he learned from Mrs Morrison at school was reinforced by Tiffany at home. Every night they practised together, and Jonas's reading and writing skills were improving daily. Best of all, the boy was becoming more confident all the time.

'I'm not yet as good as the other kids,' he said, but not unhappily.

'You will be. Remember when I promised you that you'd read as well as anyone in your class?'

'Yes...'

'Well, you're getting there now, you're doing a little better every day.' Tiffany touched his hand affectionately. 'You've worked very hard, but it's been worth it, hasn't it?'

'I guess so.'

'It's important to be able to read, Jonas. So much depends on it. I told you once that I had a friend who had a similar problem—he never did learn to read or write properly.'

'Why not, Tiffany? If I could learn, why couldn't he?'

'I'm sure he would have, if he'd had the right teacher. When he was your age, people didn't know as much as they do today about reading difficulties.'

'Was your friend ashamed that he couldn't read?' Jonas asked curiously.

'So ashamed that he couldn't bear the thought of his family and his friends knowing the truth about him. I don't think it would have mattered if they had, but *he* thought it did. He left home when he was quite young, and——'

'Never came back,' a new voice said.

Tiffany and Jonas jerked around. A tall man was standing in the doorway.

'How much did you hear, Mark?' Tiffany demanded, when she could speak.

'A fair bit. You're very lucky, Jonas. Thanks to Tiffany you won't have the problems a man called Andrew Donaldson had.'

Tiffany was shaking as she turned to the boy. 'I think we've done enough for today, Jonas. Why don't you take your books now, and we'll practise again tomorrow?'

Jonas took a few seconds to gather his things, giving Tiffany time to regain some measure of composure. When Jonas had left the kitchen, she stood up.

'You could have let me know you were eavesdropping, Mark.'

'And miss such a fascinating conversation? Not on your sweet life! Would you have spoken so freely if you'd known I were here?'

'No...'

'There you are.'

'You're totally unscrupulous,' she accused.

'Are you any better?' His eyes were shuttered. 'Don't you think I should have known about Andrew? Why didn't you tell me, Tiffany?'

'I couldn't.'

'Why not?'

'I promised him that I wouldn't.'

Mark's head lifted, his eyes lighting with sudden comprehension. 'So that's it!'

Tiffany's throat was dry. 'I shouldn't be talking about him even now,' she said tensely. 'By the way, you haven't told me what brought you here today.'

'Actually, I came to talk about Andrew,' Mark said quietly.

Tiffany looked at him bitterly. 'Some things never change. What else have you discovered? What new and terrible deed have I committed now?'

'I came to ask you about Andrew's reading problems.'

She stared at him incredulously. 'That isn't possible.'

'Why not?'

'You didn't know there was a problem until now. Until you heard me talking to Jonas.'

'I did know,' Mark said.

'I don't understand!'

'All along something didn't seem right. I was dumbfounded when you came walking into my office that first time. I couldn't believe that the lovely girl I'd just met in the street was the woman who had managed somehow to become the sole beneficiary of Andrew's estate.'

'You were so sure I had manipulated him.'

'It did seem that way at the start. But I got to know you, and I began to realise there had to be another explanation. I'm a good enough judge of people to know you weren't the conniving sort. And all the while I was becoming more and more attracted to you. I even . . .' A muscle moved in his throat.

He had spoken in a similar vein on the day he'd accused her of telling Andrew's lawyer how to draw Andrew's will. Then too he had stopped his last thought.

'Mark . . .' Tiffany whispered.

'We'll get to that, darling,' he said raggedly.

Darling? The endearment was unnerving.

'There are other things I have to say to you first.'

Darling... That was the bit Tiffany wanted to hear about, but Mark was speaking once more, and she forced herself to be patient.

'I saw how hard you worked, Tiffany. You didn't have the profile of a gold-digger, an opportunist, a woman only out to get whatever she could.'

She lifted her chin at him. 'That's what you say now, but you kept doubting me.'

'I'm a lawyer, Tiffany. I have responsibilities and I had to remember the facts.'

'You could have trusted me.'

'I wanted to. Believe it or not, there was a level on which I did trust you, but you must admit that you never gave me a fair chance. Whenever I asked you why you handled all Andrew's affairs, you always brushed me off.'

'I couldn't tell you the truth, Mark.'

'Because you'd given Andrew a promise?'

She was shaking. 'Yes...'

'There are things I've learned for myself, Tiffany, so you can talk to me now without being disloyal.'

'Mark...'

'Andrew didn't want anyone to know about his problem.'

'Yes...'

'Why not, Tiffany? It was nothing to be ashamed of.'

'That's what I kept telling him, but he didn't believe me.' Unable to shake off a sense of disloyalty, Tiffany's voice was low with distress. 'In England it didn't matter—there he was a success. But Zimbabwe was different. He would have been mortified if his family had known the truth.'

Mark's hands cupped her face. 'And so you made him a promise. A very difficult promise, as it turned out. But, being you, you kept it.' His voice was so odd.

'It really was very difficult at times,' Tiffany said through stiff lips. 'Never more so than when you found my handwritten notes.'

'It was a shock,' Mark admitted.

'That's when everything you'd thought about me at the start made sense after all.'

'For a while.'

'I don't understand...'

'There was always that feeling that there was something I didn't know. That you were keeping something from me. I decided to do some investigating.'

Tiffany tensed, without quite knowing why.

'I wasn't sure what I was looking for, so at first my quest was haphazard. I sought out people who'd known Andrew: family, neighbours, old classmates with whom he'd gone to school or played sport. And slowly a picture emerged of a boy who'd been troubled and a little insecure. A lover of animals, especially horses. Great at cricket and rugby, but miserable at school. The break came when I met the son of one of Andrew's teachers. Apparently the father had been an inveterate hoarder, and the son gave me boxes and boxes of the old man's papers. I sifted through them until I found what I was looking for.'

'What was that?' Tiffany asked, and held her breath as she waited for Mark's answer.

'An ancient notebook of Andrew's. He'd have been about fourteen at the time he wrote in it.' Mark stopped. 'I'm sure you can guess the rest.'

'You saw the way he wrote,' Tiffany said in a low voice.

'Upside down. The letters muddled and badly formed. The writing of a very young child.'

'That's when you understood.'

'Correct. So you see, rose nymph, you didn't break any promises. Hearing you talk to Jonas merely confirmed what I already knew.'

'Andrew wanted me to make those notes for the lawyer,' Tiffany said. She felt as if a huge weight had been taken from her shoulders, it was such a relief that she could talk at last. 'I didn't want to be his beneficiary, I felt his estate should go to his family. He insisted, Mark.'

'I understand that now. Andrew's family do too. By the way, they want to meet you, Tiffany. They feel rotten about the barbecue, about the way they let you down at the last moment. They want to meet you, and soon. They're worried that they might have left it too late.'

'I'd like to meet them too.'

'You're a generous girl, Tiffany. I understand how Andrew must have felt about you.' Mark's voice had grown husky. 'He couldn't have helped loving you.'

'He was never more than a friend,' Tiffany protested unsteadily.

'Even so,' Mark said, as he put out his arms and drew her to him. His sweater was rough against her cheeks, and she felt his lips in her hair.

Without loosening his arms, he lifted his head after a few minutes. 'God, I've missed you, Tiffany. Do you know what hell it was seeing you with that swine Sawyer?'

Tiffany laughed as she leaned a little away from him too. 'I think you made your feelings clear.' There was the shadow of a bruise beneath his eyes, a scratch above his lips. She touched both spots gently. 'You're looking a little the worse for wear, Mark. Did Brent do that?'

'He did.' Mark grinned down at her, his eyes alive with devilment. 'However, I'm happy to report that he looks worse than I do.'

'Two supposedly civilised men acting like a pair of stupid kids. Have you any idea how mad I was with you both? I couldn't believe that you'd fight over me.'

'Sorry to disappoint you, rose nymph, but that fight wasn't just over you, though it's true that it started that way. You might say it was a long time coming.'

'Are you telling me that when Brent jumped into the pool and slugged you, he wasn't defending the honour of his girl?'

'Honour? Brent Sawyer doesn't know the meaning of the word. You didn't really think he was serious about you, did you, Tiffany?'

This was not the time to tell Mark that a bruised and surprisingly silent Brent had appeared at the stables a few days after the party to tell her that he had made other arrangements for his horse.

'Not for a moment,' she said. 'I knew you'd been dying to get at each other's throats.'

'Actually, in my case, that's only half right. I really was fighting for my girl as well for myself.'

Tiffany grew very still as she waited for Mark to elaborate.

'Why did you invite him to the party?' he asked instead.

'I didn't want to go alone.'

'You could have asked me.'

'You were with Clarissa.'

'I can see that you might have thought that,' Mark said slowly.

'You weren't with her?' Tiffany asked disbelievingly.

'No.'

'She never left your side.'

'That's Clarissa's way.'

'I got the feeling you were very close.'

'We were never more than good friends, Tiffany. Oh, there was a time long ago when we talked about marriage, but never seriously. Clarissa knew that I didn't love her.'

But the other woman had wanted Mark as more than a friend, Tiffany thought.

'She knew that things had changed,' he said. 'She knew how angry I was with her for ruining your party. I told her all about you.'

'What about me?'

'That you were my girl.'

That expression again.

She looked up at him. 'Am I your girl, Mark?'

'Don't you know that, my darling? You've been my girl since the moment I saw you with the dried roses in your hair, laughing in the street. Not in the least upset that the cyclist had knocked you down, just treating the whole thing as a joke. *That* was when I fell in love with you.'

'*What are you saying*?'

'I love you, my darling. There was never a time when I didn't love you. That was what made doubting you such hell. Can you ever forgive me for not trusting you?'

'I'll have to work very hard at it,' she teased him, but huskily, as her heart beat a tattoo of joy inside her chest.

'You'll have a lifetime in which to do it.' He drew her towards him once more. 'I'm asking you to marry me. Will you, darling?'

'I love you too, Mark.'

'Is that a yes?'

'It is, my darling,' she said.

He looked down at her, his eyes warm with wonderment and love. 'In case you're wondering, we can keep two homes. My house in the city can be our home during the week, and we can live out here at the weekends. You'll be able to keep on with the stables.'

He kissed her then, long, hard, tenderly. Her arms went around his neck and she was kissing him too, with all the love and passion that was in her. He picked her up in his arms and carried her to the bedroom, and put her down on the bed. And then he was kissing her again.

'I want you,' he said, when he lifted his head to draw breath.

'You have me, darling.'

'I want you to be my wife. I want to love you, and cherish you, I want to make up to you for all the unhappiness I caused you. I want us to have children who look just like you. Next week, Tiffany?'

'So soon?' she teased.

'For two people whose future was written in the stars,' he told her, 'it can't be soon enough.'

Join the festivities as Mills & Boon celebrates Temptation's tenth anniversary in February 1995.

There's a whole host of in-book competitions and special offers with some great prizes to be won–watch this space for more details!

In March, we have a sizzling new mini-series Lost Loves about love lost...love found. And, of course, the Temptation range continues to offer you fun, sensual exciting stories all year round.

After ten tempting years, nobody can resist

Temptation 10th anniversary